LOVE & BETRAYAL

SOME THINGS ARE WORTH DYING FOR

BY

REGINALD J. GIST

REGINALD GIST

A T&P Publishing Book/Published by arrangement with author.

Printing History

First Printing: December 2015

Copyright 2015 by Reginald Gist

Cover Design and production: Larry Moore

ISBN: 978-0-9913581-1-3

Printed in the United States

DEDICATION

I would like to take this time to dedicate this work of art to all the fallen soldiers who lost their lives to the streets. Ya'll will never be forgotten.

R.I.H CHARLES O'NEAL

WE MAKING HISTORY!

ACKNOWLEDGMENT

I would like to acknowledge all my readers and supporters that bought this book or any other novels provided by T &P Publishing. Thanks to you...WE MAKING HISTORY!!

CHAPTER ONE

"Sir, please drop your weapon! Now!" Detective Freeman shouted over the loud entertainment system.

The black male known as Terrance stared with tears in his eyes at the detectives and the other officers as he held his chrome .38 Cali snub nose towards the ground.

"Sir, please drop your weapon now or we'll be forced to help you," the lead detective shouted again.

With a body lying on the couch bleeding from a single gunshot wound to the head and another suffering from two quick shots to the neck and stomach, Terrance reflects on the last few moments of his life as he quickly places the gun inside his mouth and pulls the trigger.

The detective watched in horror as the large framed man dropped to the floor, lifeless. The officers rushed to remove the gun from the suspects hand and to check for any vitals. Though it was apparent to them all that they would find none.

Detective Freeman and his partner Detective Ross walked over to the other body that lied on the couch to see if they could find any identification, when suddenly they heard a very faint moan coming from somewhere in the house.

"Secure the scene and nobody touch anything until C.S.I gets here, "Det. Ross commanded. "Hey you two," he said motioning to two officers, "Follow me inside."

They headed upstairs with caution to find the source of the moan. The officers made sure they were clear before entering the small bedroom. Once there, they noticed a young black female lying on the floor holding her stomach, while a stream of blood ran down her neck.

The uniformed officer yelled, "We have a live one. Call an ambulance, now!"

The detectives both rushed to her side to comfort her while they waited on the EMT's to arrive. It was apparent that something had gone totally wrong in this house.

"It's ok sweetie. Hang in there. Just try to stay calm. Help is on the way, just keep breathing," Det. Ross whispered to the young girl.

The scene quickly became chaotic as people rushed through the house looking for towels to help stop the bleeding. Finally after several minutes the ambulance arrived and she was transported into the vehicle on a stretcher.

"I'll ride along with her in case she pulls through," Det. Ross told his partner.

"Ok, I'll stay here and try to keep the scene from being contaminated, until CSI gets here to investigate," Det. Freeman replied.

Once the ambulance pulled off Freeman walked through the newly built tri-level house. He noticed pictures of the two victims and realized they were a couple and had been for several years according to their high school prom pictures.

His thoughts were interrupted by the uniformed officer, "Excuse me, sir. The investigators are here."

"Great," he said as he stepped aside and allowed the female investigator to enter.

She spoke and then started her procedure. She took her time looking over the scene, marking bullet shells and examining blood spatter marks. She came back shortly with the victim's identification and her laptop in her hand.

"Well?" Freeman asked impatiently.

"Well the gentleman on the couch who suffered from a direct gunshot to the front of his skull is named Joey Anderson. He was twenty six years old and was born here in the city. The other young man suffered what seems to be a self-inflicted gunshot wound through the mouth is Terrance Upshaw. He was twenty-two and was born and raised in Miami," she finished.

She was packing her bag as Freeman shook his head at the bloody scene. "Such a shame. So young and now so dead."

Freeman was a father of two and had been on the police force for twenty-three years, longer than the young man had been alive. With two daughters close to the same age, it still stung whenever he saw things like this. He had witnessed everything from suicides, murders and kidnappings. His record of solving cases was impeccable and he was highly respected on the force, but this case was extremely difficult for him.

If the young lady didn't survive then they were at ground zero in the investigation.

"Were there any drugs or money on their persons?" he asked her.

"Only small bills and credit cards on the victim and several thousand dollars on the perp."

"Hmmmm, do a clean sweep of the vehicles out front and I'm gonna call to check on the girl," he said. "Let's get this shit cleaned up and after the coroners leave, seal it up,"

He stepped out on the front porch and immediately reached for a cigarette inside the pocket of his blazer. He lit it up then called his partner. After a few rings, he picked up, "Freeman, what's up?"

"Just finishing up at the scene, checking in with you. How is the girl?"

"Well as of now she's in surgery and still fighting for her life. The ride over wasn't pleasant at all and I don't think she is going to make it. IF she does, I doubt if she'll be able to tell us anything," Ross said.

"Fuck! Did you get an ID?" Freeman barked into the phone between drags on his cigarette.

"Her name is Stacy Moore and she's twenty-five and apparently a graduate of Cass Tech High school says her Alumni Association card."

"Ok, let's contact the families and see if we can piece this shit together before the press gets a hold to it. I'll catch you back at headquarters later," he said hanging up the phone. He threw the cigarette butt on the ground and stepped on it.

After Ross was able to catch up with Stacy's mother and deliver the news no mother wants to hear, she raced up to the hospital to check on her daughter. She explained that Stacy lived with her fiancé Joey for several years but she had never heard of the other guy.

They were still talking when the doctor walked in Mrs. Moore immediately pummeled him with a million questions, "How is she? Is she still alive?"

The doctor, used to dealing with distraught family members, waited patiently for her to calm down then explained, "Your daughter is out of surgery, but is in critical condition. We removed one bullet from her stomach but it tore through multiple layers of intestine and damaged her ovaries, which we had to remove. Also we removed a bullet from her neck that shattered the back reptilian gland which stopped her from breathing due to the lack of oxygen."

Mrs. Moore listened intently while tears streamed down her face. The doctor continued, "She's a strong girl and full recovery is likely but we have to watch her until she regains consciousness."

Mrs. Moore let out a huge sigh of relief before the doctor said, "If she does pull through, I'm afraid that her memory might be delayed and/or permanently damaged, we have to wait and see, unfortunately."

"Can I see her?"

"Yes, I'll take you back," he said leading her and the detective back to the room where Stacy was resting. "She is in the best care here at D.M.C. I'll give you a few minutes but she needs to rest," he said turning to leave.

"Thank you so much for taking care of her," Mrs. Moore said.

Det. Ross stayed at the door while Stacy's mother sat at the side of the hospital bed. He really hoped that she would come to. Her explanation of the events that had taken place was vital to them solving this case. He had gotten a little bit of information from her mom about the two victims, but the third one was a mystery to the both of them.

He excused himself, giving Mrs. Moore some time alone with Stacy. Outside the room he dialed his partner to let him know the latest news on the surviving victim.

"Ok stay with the family while I run these names through the system. We still haven't contacted the shooters family as of now, but we're on it. The boyfriend's family is at the morgue and will be in for an interview shortly. I'll see you back at the station," Det. Freeman said. Then he remembered, "Oh by the way, there was forced entry at the scene. Yeah, I know it gets crazier by the minute. Catch you later, man."

Ross hung up his cell phone processing the information his partner had given him when he heard a scream. Mrs. Moore was screaming for a doctor or nurse when he rushed back into the room.

"She opened her eyes and reached for me!!" she screamed. "Then I think she passed out! Please get the doctor!"

By then the nurses were rushing into the room and the doctor had been paged. Both Mrs. Moore and the

Detective stepped back hoping for the best for the young lady who had survived something so awful.

CHAPTER TWO

Waking up and seeing the woman by her bedside had been too much for Stacy. She was afraid because she no idea where she was or who the lady was. She had tried her best to speak or remember something, but the pain was too much as she slipped back into her coma searching for answers.

She drifted under the darkness of the coma and reminisced about her teenage years. At thirteen her vision and talent became drawing and paintings. Everyone admired her work and predicted she was a gifted child. At ten her father had been killed in a local bar over a drug deal gone sour. She knew he was a bad boy but she loved him and her mother with all her heart. As the only child, her life felt empty, so after her father passed she turned to her best friend Kim for comfort and advice.

They both attended Cass Tech High School and were both honor roll students. Her dad would have been so proud of her if he was alive. Her mother on the other hand was strict and always stayed close to act as a guide and counselor throughout life.

As she had gotten older, she had become more in tuned with her artwork, school and boys. At sixteen, she stood at a modest five feet 8 inches and could pass for a model. Her shapely body and cocoa brown skin coupled with her long thick hair hanging down her back put her at the top of the most wanted list in Cass. Kim was a shorter, light skinned version of her. Her short bouncy bob cut and green eyes catapulted her right next to Stacy on the list.

They did everything together and promised each other that they would always be best friends no matter what. They even vowed to keep their virginity until marriage. Growing up on the west side of Detroit made this a challenge along with other temptations that presented themselves.

On their ways to school one day while they were catching the Grand River bus, they stopped at the gas station to grab a few snacks and bumped into a few boys from their school.

"What's up, Stacy?" asked the one named Joey who everyone called J-Rock.

"Nothing much, just getting a few thing before school," she replied while holding up a handful of junk food.

"What's up Kim? You ain't speaking?" the other boy, Rondo asked.

"Boy chill, I'm just checking ya'll out," she said with a laugh.

"Why you ain't called me yet? You acting funny," Joey asked Stacy.

"Boy, you tripping. You know you are all over the place," she said smiling at the tall boy with dark chocolate colored skin and dimples as deep as pot holes.

"Damn, girl. Ya need to give your boy Joey one shot at the title," he said.

"Yeah and you should give me a second chance," Rondo hollered at Kim.

Kim slowly rolled her eyes at him. They had hooked up before but he couldn't live down his reputation as a ladies man. Eventually they broke off their teenage love and he had wanted her back ever since, especially because they hadn't had sex.

Joey had attended Cass Tech last year, but had been kicked out for having drugs in his locker and on school grounds. Both he and Rondo attended Redford High School now and they would catch the girls at the bus stop on Grand River and Evergreen every now and then. J-Rock and Rondo still sold drugs but still realized that their education was a priority.

"Why don't you call me tonight," Joey asked Stacy.

Even though she knew he was a bad boy, she truly found him irresistible. "Yeah, I got your number. I'll text you after school, mayyyybbeee!" she teased.

"Damn, you just made a nigga day, shorty. Alight 'til later," he said.

'Let's go nigga! The bus coming," Rondo yelled. "Byyyeee Kimmy," he said jokingly walking across the street to the bus headed west on Grand River.

She shook her head and laughed.

"Man, I really like girlie. She been hot since open enrollment," J-Rock said on the short bus ride.

"Yeah, she straight but her and Kim be on that "no fucking" bullshit. That's why me and her stopped talking. You know me, if you ain't fucking then I'm trucking the hell on," Rondo spoke with a serious look on his face.

"That's cool, but you gotta be patient with these kinds of girls. I use to fuck with Stacy in the hallway every day and she was just about to crack when they found that ounce in my damn coat and kicked me out. It's cool though cause now I'm in the car and my money game getting up, ya dig?"

All day in school Stacy daydreamed about her Dad, who she missed so much. Then her thoughts wandered to that morning when she had seen Joey. She liked him and found him attractive but something about him reminded her of her Dad.

"Ok class, pass your papers up to the front and you guys have a safe weekend. I'll see you all on Monday and be prepared for the math quiz!" the teacher yelled over the hoard of kids making their way to the door.

Stacy snapped out of her thoughts as she heard the teacher's raspy voice and all the kids getting up out of their seats. Kim was waiting for her at the door with her cell phone in hand. "Hey, best friend let's get out of here before the bus gets too crowded. It's the weekend and we need to hit the mall to grab a few outfits for Tina's party at Mr. Nick's," she said smiling.

"Right, let me hurry up and put these books up in my locker. T.G.I.F and you know Fairlane is going to be jumping with all kinds of cuties," Stacy said walking towards her locker.

They were right as the mall was jammed packed as they surveyed the stores and the young men lingering around the mall.

"So what's really the deal with you and Joey, girl? He been on your heels since last year and I know you are feeling him," Kim said as they walked passed Auntie Annie's. They both waved to a girl that went to their school that worked there.

"He's cool. It's just that whole dope boy thing that scares me. I've seen how they change from good to bad in a heartbeat. I don't want my first boyfriend or virginity to be taken lightly. I want it to be special girl, don't you?"

"Of course, that's why Rondo's ass stop messing with me. He wanted to move too fast but I wanted more. I wanted to at least love the nigga I give this special treatment too," Kim responded laughing.

"I know that's right, in fact when I get home I'll text Joey to see where his head is at," Stacy said while eating a piece of cheesecake. They finished shopping and headed home.

Later that night while she watched something on BET, she decided to text Joey.

: What's up stranger? As a woman I kept my word and I'm reaching out to see what's on ya mind. If ya not 2 busy feel free to text back or call.

She sat the phone down and went back to watching her program.

J-Rock felt his phone vibrating in his pocket as he sat in his boy's truck on the block. "Oh shit, shorty hit me up." He read the short text and texted back.

: It must be my lucky day. Thanks for getting at me sexy. I'm on the block for another hour or so but I promise I will hit you back before 11. Is that ok?

"Damn, he got back quick. I like that," Stacy thought to herself as she read the text. She called Kim and they talked until 11 that night.

"Alright ya'll, I'll catch up with ya'll later. Yo, Rondo don't forget I'll pick you up tomorrow at nine to hit the party up," J-Rock shouted over the loud sound system.

"Cool," Rondo said as he rolled up the window and drove off.

As soon as J-Rock entered his house he spoke to his mom and ran to his room. He turned on his radio and let the Quiet Storm play low, then pulled out his cell to call Stacy.

The phone rang a few times before a half-sleep Stacy answered, "Hello?"

"What's up shorty, my bad for calling a little late. Things ran behind schedule, but I did rush home to talk to you before bed," J-Rock said in his sexiest voice.

"It's cool; I was just laying here letting the TV watch me while I drew a little."

"Oh, you draw, huh? That's cute."

"Yeah, ever since I was ten I've loved arts and crafts. So drawing became a hobby and a way to express myself."

"Maybe one day I'll get to see your artwork," he slid in.

"Maybe, we'll see," again she spoke back.

After about an hour of conversation it was clear that they were feeling each other. They found out that they both knew Tina and had planned on going to her party.

"Yeah, I'll be there until my curfew. My mom be on my head she already told me to be in the house by 1 a.m.," she replied with an attitude.

"Damn, it ain't over until two, but hey she has to protect her baby. It's cool though, hopefully I'll see you and maybe you save a non-dancing nigga, a dance or two."

"Tell your boy don't be tripping if Kim don't give him no action. You already know how crazy he can get."

"Don't worry I'll have him under control, trust me," he switched the topic quickly, "I really enjoyed talking to you, it's about time you gave me a chance. Get you some rest and hopefully I'll see you tomorrow at the party."

"Yeah that will be cool. Thanks for the convo, I'll catch up with you at the party. I'll be the baddest chick in the house. Night, night," she flirted and hung up the phone.

J-Rock looked at the phone with a smile on his face. "Yeah, that's what's up," he said to himself.

CHAPTER THREE

Mr. Nicks was packed from wall to wall. The line outside was around the corner as teenagers stood to enter the huge club. It was mid-May and the weather was getting warmer. Inside the club the loud system blasted Little Wayne and T-Pain. In the corner J-Rock and his Fenkell Ave crew surveyed the crowd and across the room Stacy, Kim and their friends were posted in another corner.

When their jam came on the girls all headed to the floor as the fellas watched. They each picked a girl and then pounced on them like lions after prey. Joey approached the dance floor and pull up behind Stacy, who was rocking a low cut shirt that read 'The Wifey Type" and some tight Guess jeans.

"What up doe Shorty, can I get that dance now?" he said in her ear.

"Boy you crazy! You don't even know how to dance, but show me what you got," she joked. She admired Joey as he looked fresh to def in his Coogi jogging suit and Gator gym shoes.

Everyone watched as they danced for several songs until a slow jam came on.

"You lied Joey," she whispered in his ear as he held her close, "You're a little touchy feely but you alright."

"Ya, know I do what I can do. Ya dig?"

Stacy was in heaven as they danced to Mint Condition's *Pretty Brown Eyes*.

"You know I usually don't slow dance but you looking so fly, I had to break the code," J-Rock said softly in her ear as he watched all the kids who didn't have a dance partner clear the dance floor.

Stacy just smiled as they rocked to the rhythm as both of their crews watched them from the sidelines. She felt his arms around her waist and somehow felt safe right at that moment. She started thinking Joey just might be the one. She loved everything about him, his height, beautiful dark smooth skin and his swagger was on ten. She leaned in closer, breathing in his Drakkar cologne and didn't want the song to end.

J-Rock looked at his watch and saw that time was winding down for them. It was already 12:30 and he knew she had to be in by 1 so he wanted some time for them to kick it. When the song ended he grabbed her hand and led her over to an empty table so that they could talk.

Kim and Rondo walked over to the table where they were sitting.

"Ya'll are pretty lovey-dovey don't you think?" Kim said with a smile.

"Yeah, we gon' let ya'll chill. Just holla when you ready to leave cause you know Mom Dukes is on her head," Rondo yelled over the music.

"Boy, shut up and let's get something to drink. Don't worry I got this nigga, Joey. We'll be over at the picture booth, ya'll," Kim said dragging Rondo away.

'Those two right there are funny as hell," J-Rock said.

"Tell me about it. One day they hate each other and then the next they are BFF's," she responded.

They engaged in conversation for a few more minutes before they decided to leave. Joey's curfew was only a half hour after hers so they had to get going. While the party was still going the four of them exited the club and headed for their cars outside.

Kim had borrowed her brothers Honda Accord while the boys rode in J-Rock's father's F-250 truck. Standing at the side of the Honda everyone exchanged hugs and said their good-bye.

"What's up with you and I getting together for a one on one?" J-Rock said to Stacy.

"Oh, you asking me out on a date Mr. Gangsta?"

"I really enjoyed your company and conversation the past few days, so I figured that it would be nice to chill out with you by ourselves. Next weekend I got my Pop's ride and I would like to take you out to eat and to check out that new King of Comedy movie," he said gazing into her eyes.

"I'll call you and let you know. Stay ya butt outta trouble and I'll talk to you later, ok?" she said trying to contain her happiness inside.

Rondo was already in the car complaining that he wanted to stop at the Coney Island before they went in. So

J-Rock laughed and said, "He tripping. Ya'll be safe and we'll catch up with ya'll later on tomorrow."

Driving home Kim added, "J-Rock on you tough, girl! If he keeps that up he might get that nookie!"

"You so silly girl. He cooler than I thought and he asked me out next weekend. What you think about that?"

"He cool and by the way ya'll was chilling he might be a nice cat. Shit he might be able to teach Rondo's ass some game," Kim responded laughing.

When Stacy got in she took a quick shower and was getting ready for bed when she noticed a text from Joey on her phone.

:You were on my mind and I just wanted to send you a good night kiss thru a text. Sweet dreams and I hope u take me up on that date

Stacy quickly responded:

:How cute I'm still on ya mind. Kisses back to you and I'll holla at ya soon!

She laid back in the bed and thought of how nice it would be to go out with Mr. Tall, Dark & Handsome.

CHAPTER FOUR

Over the next few weeks, Stacy and J-Rock talked and texted every night. They didn't see each other on the bus route but they made sure they communicated every day. Each day the conversations got deeper and eventually she gave in and accepted his invitation to a date.

That Saturday Joey picked her up from her house. Mrs. Moore and had approved he going out as long as she met the young man and saw his driver's license and copied down his address.

J-Rock looked nice in his Nautica jogging suit with a pair of A.C.G's for footwear. Stacy had a Baby Phat jean outfit and some Gucci strap sandals. After the pick-up, they headed to J-Alexander's for dinner.

After they were seated they both looked over the menu and were ready to order when the waiter reappeared. J-Rock took the liberty of ordering for Stacy. "The lady will be having the Chicken Fettuccini with a splash of lemon garlic and I'll have the Steak Maui, medium well with mashed potatoes."

Stacy watched as the waiter thanked him and took the menus. "Oh, you know you just too smooth, huh?" she said.

"Hey, I know what my lady wants and I always give her what she needs."

"Well, I hope I like it Mr. Big Shot. I have to admit that got you a few extra brownie points," she said softly punching in the arm.

After dinner they headed to the Star Theater in Southfield. They both enjoyed the movie and he made sure to have her home on time.

"I really enjoyed dinner and the movie, Joey," Stacy said as they neared her block. "Cedric the Entertainer is a damn fool."

"He is crazy as hell," J-Rock agreed. "I'm glad you enjoyed yourself."

"You ain't as bad as the streets say," she said in a soft voice.

"Oh, I'm still bad I just know how to treat a lady," he laughed. "I had fun too, so hopefully we can do it again and soon."

He pulled up to her house and said, "So, can I walk you to the door?"

"Nah, I'm cool. My mom is probably posted in the window watching our every move," she said.

J-Rock tried to lean over to get a quick kiss but she was quicker. "I don't kiss and I haven't had sex, so hopefully you can respect that and let me open up on my terms and in my own time, gangsta." She got out and closed the truck door but not before saying, "Next date is on me."

J-Rock was still reeling from her first statement but gathered himself enough to say, "Cool, get some rest and holla at me when you get free."

He pulled off and laughed. He had to respect her. She was straight forward about what she wanted and what she was willing to put up with.

He was a street nigga but not at heart. This part of his life had been forced on him. His father had been involved in the street for as long as J-Rock had been alive. Coming up J-Rock had witnessed every level of the game and learned a lot from the streets. The love his father had for his mother showed him how to always treat a lady. His mother took good care of the house and his Dad never brought the street life home with him.

J-Rock observed the commitment that his father showed his mother and how he protected her and her feelings, because she deserved it. He vowed that he would always respect women and whoever he loved would have the same traits as his mother. He could see some of those traits in Stacy already. But there was also another side to J-Rock that he had inherited from his father, who was the head of the Fenkell Ave. Boys. He was an up and coming underboss and he took that as serious as anything else.

They continued to talk and text after that date and they spent countless hours on the phone until a bond was quickly formed. J-Rock had to admit that Stacy was really keeping his interest unlike other girls that he had dated.

They didn't see each other over the next few weeks because the change of their school schedules and activities, but Stacy had asked him was he ready for their next date because she had something special planned. Of course, he was ready! There were only a few weeks until summertime and this date she wanted to be special all around....

CHAPTER FIVE

On Saturday Kim helped Stacy prepare for her date. "Girl your hair is the bomb and those shoes are fly as hell," she said as she sat on Stacy's bed watching her friend get dressed.

"Well Joey has been really cool so I wanted to dress a little cute for the art show," Stacy said twirling in front of the mirror.

"Umm-hmm, ya'll getting pretty close and you got that look," Kim teased.

"Don't even go there, girl. He is special but he has a long way to go."

"Whatever," Kim rolled her eyes.

"Stop hating! I have to finish up, he'll be here in a minute."

Her phone rang as soon as she finished that sentence, it was J-Rock telling her he was outside.

"Ok, I'll be out in about five minutes. Kim is fixing my hair," Stacy replied.

"Cool, tell Kim I said what up with her crazy ass," he said.

It was a beautiful day and the weather was cooperating for the date, at a breezy 85 degrees. The light blue sundress she wore blew in the breeze as she walked to the car. Joey watched as she glided to the car as her slim frame shown through the thin sundress.

"Have fun!" Kim yelled out the door. "J-Rock you betta be nice punk!"

He ignored Kim and greeted Stacy, "Hey beautiful."

"Hey, I hope you are ready for a change of environment. I love art and thought I would share a little of my world with you."

"I'm down for something new, it sounds like fun," he answered.

The art show was beautiful and had they looked at every display. There were paintings by famous artist and statues from all over the world. J-Rock listened while Stacy explained every piece in detail. He was so fascinated by her. She really knew her stuff and that alone kept the date interesting.

After a few hours of walking around the art fair, they decided to call it a day and go get something to eat. Stacy suggest the soul food restaurant, Southern Fires, in downtown Detroit.

The ride there was relaxing as Joey text and jammed to his latest Hot Trax's cd's. Once the truck was handed over to the valet, they entered the place looking like a couple. J-Rock noticed a lot of up and coming gangsta's who gave a special salute to show respect to his gang. He saluted back as they took a seat by the window.

"Who is that?" Stacy asked.

"Just a few of my Dad's friends," he said.

"I love this place. The food is so good. So can I order for you this time, Gangsta?"

"Fasho, I trust you. Just please no pork, that shit messes with my stomach," he smiled and rubbed his stomach.

When the waiter arrived, Stacy order herself a Surf and Turf entrée and ordered Joey a Charbroiled New York stripe butterflied with Mac and cheese and yams.

"Look at you getting your big girl on," he teased.

The food was wonderful as they talked and laughed and talked about people. It was only 9 pm when they finished and they still had a few hours to kill before she had to be home.

She shot Kim a quick text:

:Having a ball! Will call you later with details. Love ya!

She called her Mom just to let her know that she ok and of course she reminded Stacy of her curfew. While they waited for the valet to pull the truck up, Joey suggested they go chill at his brother's town house for a few hours since he was gone and they were close by.

She agreed and shortly after that they pulled into the parking garage off of Jefferson Ave.

"This is really nice," she said looking around. "Yeah, I could get used to house like this."

"Yeah, my brother is a street nigga and this is crib that Pop's got him for his hard work," J-Rock said while looking around.

"This is how I need to be living after school," she said.

"Yeah he spoiled as hell. Let's chill in the back den where the big screen is at," he suggested leading her to the back.

"What kind of work does your Dad do, Joey?"

"He runs a real estate company but he is well connected in the streets. When I'm not in school, I'm usually earning my money doing as he says or ask."

"Sounds like you set for life, if you ask me," she said.

"I guess but I want to be my own boss, someday."

"You will just keep working hard, baby."

J-Rock reached for the remote and turned on Poetic Justice on the huge screen. They sat on the couch next to each other while the movie played. He really like Stacy a lot and wanted to make her his main chick. He had been around his share of females and wasn't a virgin, as a matter fact he had quite a bit of experience. The street life and his older brother allowed him to view game up close and personal. The only problem was he wasn't sure if Stacy was into him the same. She had already made it clear that she wasn't trying to have sex but he had to test her no kissing rule.

"Can I rub your shoulders, Ms. Thang?" he asked.

Stacy looked over at him. She was really feeling him and wanted him to herself. She had heard rumors of how violent he was in the street and that he ran with the Fenkell Boys under his dad's leadership. This actually turned her on because he was so humble, sweet and mature for his age. She felt a sense of protection when they were together and her guard was completely down when she was around him.

"You can rub my shoulders Joey. Do you mind if I take my shoes off? My feet are killing me."

Slowly she leaned back unto him as he began to massage her shoulders and back. She relaxed and enjoyed the treatment and was pleasantly surprised when he started kissing her neck. She like the feeling it gave her so she turned to meet his mouth with hers. They embraced in a kiss and she completely turned around giving him access to lay on top of her.

He eagerly complied and as he kissed her, he ran his hand up her dress to her soft spot. She was so wet her panties were moist. Once she felt his warm hand on her pussy she grabbed his wrist to control the movement and depths of his fingers.

"Be careful please Joey. You know I'm a virgin," she whispered.

The sound of those words echoed through his head as he became more careful with his touch. "I'll be gentle, baby. Let me guide you, just follow me, " he whispered back.

Slowly she relaxed as he rubbed his index finger in circles around her clit.

She could barely contain herself as she moaned while she kissed him. He continued to rotate his fingers to keep her nice and wet for the big moment.

He slid her panties down and off while raising her sundress he glanced at her beautiful untouched body. Her breast were the size of caramel apples and her skin was the color of mocha. From past experiences he knew what girls wanted and liked during sex, so he tried his best to use his knowledge to his advantage.

Looking at her bunny trail he gentle massaged her breast by slightly squeezing her nipples. Then he kissed her belly button while licking up and down her pussy lips. He ended up making fast short licks directly to her clit which was swollen from pleasure.

"Oh my God Joey! That feels so good," she moaned softly. He continued to lick faster as he inserted his fingers into her soft, wet, tight pussy. Then moments later he could feel her body vibrate as her legs raised and clamped around his head.

"I'm about to cum," she screamed as she grabbed at the sheets.

He allowed her to enjoy the after effects of her orgasm as he slid up to kiss her neck. He used that as a distraction as he moved to take her mind off the main event. With his dick in hand he positioned the tip directly in front of her pussy. Exercising patience he pushed slowly, in and out until he could feel her virgin walls opening.

She let out a small whimper and held him tighter. "It's ok, baby. Just a little more to go," he said softly helping her to relax. She bit down on her bottom lip and opened her legs more.

Several minutes later, their rhythm matched as she rolled her hips and cried. It was only ten minutes later when he felt the urge to release. He knew he couldn't do it inside of her so he pulled out.

She laid there feeling elated at what had just happened. Feeling his muscular body on top of hers was like no other feeling she had ever felt before. She had always thought it would be unbearable but he had taken his time and worked with her.

He led her to the bathroom where they took a shower in the marble covered bathroom.

"So where do we go from here," she asked as she washed his back.

"Stacy you know my lifestyle and there is a lot you don't know about me yet. I like you a lot in fact I think I'm starting to feel the love bug biting, despite the sex. I know that we are young but I'm willing to grow up with you. This is my last year in school and I plan to start a business after I graduate. So why not try to build something with someone special. I think you trust me, so let's become a couple. What do you think?" he said turning around to face her.

"I do trust you and you took my nook-nook in the process. I've never had a boyfriend or been in love but I'm willing to learn. I have two more years left then I'm going to college to get my degree. I would love to be your lady but you gotta treat me right all the time Joey. I mean it," she said with a serious look on her face.

"Ok, I got you. A couple, we are," he said kissing her gently.

They finished up and headed to her house. When they pulled up her mother was waiting in the doorway so that killed any idea of good bye kisses.

"I'll call you later to check on you. You better go straight home boy, it's late," she demanded.

As soon as he pulled off, she ran in to call Kim before it was too late.

Kim answered on the first ring, "You better had called me. Spill it, Apollo is boring as hell!"

Stacy gave all the details of that nights event and Kim listened to every word spoken and asked questions when she could.

"You have got to be kidding me!!! I can't believe you gave it up!" Kim giggled into the phone.

"Nope and it felt so good, it didn't hurt at all. After we finished we decided to make it official and become a couple," Stacy gushed into the phone.

"Oh my God, girl you already know he is a gangsta and be selling drugs and shit. You gotta be careful with him at all time. At least I will say that he's not like Rondo so you might have gotten the better one!" Kim joked backed.

After she hung up with Kim, she texted Joey to check on him.

:Hey baby. Just checking to see if you made it home safely. I just wanted to say goodnight. Xoxoxoxo Stacy

J-Rock was sitting on his bed watching Rondo roll up a blunt. They were talking about the date and the new relationship he had committed to when he saw her text come across.

:Thanks for checking on me babe. I'm cool, at the spot with crazy ass Rondo. I had a good time and I miss you already. I'll hit you after the gym, then we can talk. Sleep tight. Love ya xoxoxox J-rizzle

Stacy laid back in her bed after she read the text and smiled to herself.

"He said he loves me," she said to herself. Seconds later she was falling asleep, on cloud nine.

CHAPTER SIX

Mrs. Moore had been at Stacy's bed side since they had brought her to the hospital and she was praying that her baby girl would wake up. She was holding Stacy's hand when she felt her hand tighten around her own. She wasn't sure if what she had felt was real but she raised her head so that she could watch it, but seconds later she felt it again.

She pushed the nurse's button over and over so that someone would come to check on her.

"Is something wrong Mrs. Moore?" the on duty nurse asked.

"She squeezed my hand. Twice! I think she trying to wake up!" the older woman yelled.

"Ok, calm down Mrs. Moore. The doctor is on his way in," the nurse said.

Minutes later the handsome doctor walked in just as the nurse checked her vitals. "Hello Mrs. Moore and Det. Ross, how are you both?" he asked. Neither of them answered so he continued. "Stacy's vital signs are still low. What you are witnessing is a dramatic stage that the body goes through during recovery. Tensing of the body or movement of the eyes just allows us to know that she is still conscious. All we can do is wait and pray for a speedy recovery. Nurse, please change the bandages and start another IV. I will come check on her later."

"Mrs. Moore, can I have a word with you outside," Det. Ross asked.

"Sure, is everything ok?" Mrs. Moore asked.

"Well I spoke with Joey's parents and they are upset as to be expected. They are seeking answers and want to meet up with you," he said.

"Well, have you gotten any leads on the guy that shot my baby?" she asked angrily?

"As of right now, no. We have issued his picture to all local precincts and some in the neighboring states. We also have the press reporting the story and asking for any tips from the public. The ID that the perp had on him was a fake, so it's becoming harder to solve the identity issue. Hopefully, Stacy will make a full recovery and then we hopefully will have all of our questions answered."

He continued, "Until then I'll let Joey's family know you are too distraught to talk right now and need more time. They are in the process of preparing for the funeral. Just remember you aren't alone in this and ya'll need each other."

"Ok, Detective you know where I'll be. Give my condolences to the family," Mrs. Moore replied through tears.

It had been five days since the murders and everyone had a lot on their minds. The detectives searched a prepared for a case that had no solid motive. They knew nothing and wondered was the young couple being robbed? They even tried the "hit" theory since Joey was a known drug dealer and an affiliate of the Fenkell Boys. If it wasn't for the silent alarm the perp would have gotten away clean. They had so many unanswered questions and little hope finding the answers. The streets had an unbreakable code of silence and the only surviving victim was in a coma and barely hanging on. They needed answers and they needed them now.

As Stacy lay motionless in her bed, her brain shied away from the pain and went into recall mode. Mrs. Moore sat vigilant at her daughter's side. She looked through old scrap books and pictures of Stacy and her artwork. Here, she would remain until her daughter woke up to explain the tragic events.

"Sleep tight baby, get your rest. God will help us through this. I know your father is watching over you, so be strong," Mrs. Moore spoke quietly.

She grabbed Stacy's hand and prayed under her breath. No reaction came from Stacy so her mother continued her mission of staying close and watching after her.

CHAPTER SEVEN

The months following their decision to become a couple went well. They did everything together from hanging out to schoolwork. J-Rock's dad had given him the truck to have sine he was graduating and he loved it. Slowly he would prepare for the summer by hustling and staying focused on his relationship.

Stacy remained the loyal companion and she supported her man's every move. He could do no wrong and Kim began to get jealous since Stacy was in love and seemingly growing up without her. They had grown up as a team but somehow it seemed she had been benched.

J-Rock and Stacy were moving at a steady pace and had no room for error. Both families had accepted their relationship and kept a close watch on them over the summer.

Summertime in the "D" put a strain on any relationship, but J-Rock and Stacy were focused. His status in the streets was growing daily. He was becoming known as that street hustler that took no shorts and gave no loans. His crew, under his father's direction were becoming a force to reckon with. They were known for setting up crack houses in neighborhoods and beating down anyone who interfered with their profit margin.

Since he was out of school, J-Rock started to set his vision on course by saving money and planning to open his own business like his dad. The real estate game was wide open and he knew exactly how to tap into it.

Being that Rondo was his right hand man and he always kept him close on staff. Rival crews wanted then and the Fenkell Boys out of business and would stop at nothing to prove their point.

Though he was in the streets he made sure Stacy was a priority. No matter how much money he made or drama that came his way he forever treated her like a queen. She stayed at the mall and never missed a major event in the city. She was known as the dope man's wifey and all respect was given.

Throughout the summer their relationship had grown to another level. He made sure that her school work and goals stayed intact along with her focus on her art and designs. She had one more year of school before she picked the college she wanted to attend. The thought of her leaving Joey behind hurt her deep inside but she had to do what was best for her. He understood and promised to continue to hold her down while she away.

One night over dinner she asked, "You know at the end of this year I'll be leaving for school, right?"

"Of course I know. I'm proud of you for sticking to your goals," he said stuffing his mouth with a piece of steak.

"What are you going to do while I'm gone?"

"What you mean?"

"I don't want you fucking with no hoes and spoiling our relationship," she said pointedly.

"Yo, chill out Boo. We good girl. I'm strictly about the cash and building my business for our future," he said slightly aggravated.

"Alright, I'm telling you no bullshitting and you better come see me all the time," she pouted.

"Wherever you go baby, trust me, I'll follow," he said soothing her.

"Until then let's just enjoy our time together. So take me home and do something to make me feel good," Stacy said while pointing to her secret spot.

They quickly exited the diner and headed to his brother's town house to chill out for a few.

Over the next few months school had started back and Stacy was aiming high to get accepted into a good college. Her art teacher suggested that she apply for a scholarship to Trudell's School of Art. The school was in New York and was recognized nationally as one of the best. She thought strongly about being so far away from home but then decided that the opportunity was worth the risk. So during the rest of the year she worked hard to keep her grades up and stayed focused.

Kim and Rondo both had decided not to go to college. Kim had a different outlook on life and allowed the streets to take her under. Ever since Stacy and Joey had gotten together, Kim had been jealous and Stacy knew it, but Kim remained a true friend. Joey didn't approve of the guys that Kim went out with because they were from rival gangs and to him that didn't show loyalty or any respect.

J-Rock continued to show Stacy support by taking her to and from school each day. He would go to art shows and purchased supplies to fund her dream. He was getting older and he had a strong sense of direction for his own life as well.

While sitting in his truck waiting for Stacy and Kim to exit school one day, a few guys from Seven Mile were out trying to catch a few girls heading home from school.

"What's up with these niggas?" Rondo asked looking at the guys.

"I don't know. Fuck them cats," he said looking for Stacy.

A few minutes later Kim and Stacy rushed out the school to the truck.

"Hey Boo. How was your day?" she said jumping in the front seat and giving him a kiss.

"Shit was cool, just missing you that's all," he answered.

They waited for Rondo to finish smoking outside the truck while he and Kim argued about who didn't call who last night.

The two Seven Mile guys had driven up close to the truck and the passenger leaned out the window, "Damn, Kim. What up? You looking good."

"No this nigga is not frontin,'" Kim thought to herself, ignoring the guy.

"Oh you can't speak cause you with these hoe ass niggas, huh?" he shouted again.

Before he could finish his statement Rondo stepped up and made Kim get in the truck, "My man, who the fuck you think you talking to nigga?!" Rondo asked.

The driver of the car leaned over and threw up a Seven Mile gang sign, while flashing a black 9mm pistol. "I'm talking to the bitch but since you cock blocking then I'm talking to you," the passenger said.

Rondo looked at J-Rock as the truck ran with the girls waiting inside. Seconds later he jumped out the truck holding his .40 caliber with the extended clip. Rondo reached for his .45 he kept in the small of his back.

At the same time the dudes in the old school had drawn their weapons and fired several shots while pulling off.

J-Rock and Rondo exchanged fire while taking cover on the side of the huge truck. School kids scattered like roaches trying to avoid being hit by any stray bullets. Bullets flew at the Chevy as it hit Grand River and sped off to the east bound freeway. No was hit in the truck once the shooting was over.

J-Rock jumped into the truck only to find Stacy in the driver's seat.

"Get in! Let's go now," she demanded.

The boys followed orders and jumped in as she drove off.

"You alright baby," J-Rock asked checking her over.

Stacy was calm but Kim was shaking from all the drama that had taken place.

"What the fuck we're ya'll thinking?" Stacy yelled. "We could have gotten killed and this is my school Joey!"

"It wasn't my fault, shit! Kim, who the fuck were those niggas?" J-Rock said putting the guns in the stash spot.

"Them niggas from Seven Mile and Greenfield J-Rock. I used to hang out with them a while ago. I'm sorry Stacy, it's not my fault," she said afraid of J-Rock.

"Girl you straight. Let's just get off the streets in this hot ass truck," Stacy said.

"Go to the spot on Oakman and we'll switch cars with Count," Rondo suggested.

"Cool, hit him up and let him know what's up," J-Rock said.

Stacy headed in that direction and they stayed with the plan. They switched cars and J-Rock got them home safely.

Later that night Stacy and J-Rock talked about the day's crazy events. He told her how happy and surprised he was to see her spring into action. She had his back and that only strengthened his love for her.

Since he knew picking her up from school in the truck would be dangerous, he kept the routine but switched to a rented Lexus until shit died down. Everyone knew that the drama wasn't over and to J-Rock it was just another day at the office. Stacy preferred that he lay low while she finished school and prepared for college.

The weeks flew by with no action as J-Rock and Rondo made money not war. Kim and Stacy were almost out of school and excited to spend their last summer together.

The incident with the Seven Mile Boys was never far from J-Rock and Rondo's minds and they were a little skeptical about the company that Kim kept. They never held a grudge but always kept a close on eye on her whenever she was around.

Three weeks before the end of school Stacy's mom ran into her room very excited.

"Honey bunch! Honey Bunch! Guess what just came in the mail?" she yelled.

"What ma? I don't know," she replied lost.

"It's a letter from the Art school in New York!"

Stacy tore open the big yellow envelope and pulled out the contents. She quickly scanned the letter looking for the words she wanted to read. "YES! They accepted me! I got accepted Ma," she said with tears of joy.

"You deserve it baby and I'm so proud of you," her mom said hugging her.

She couldn't wait to share the news with Joey and Kim. She texted Joey who was in the studio with his boy Rome. Then she called Kim who was at the nail shop.

"Hey Stacy what's up?" Kim answered.

"I got accepted to the Art School," she said happily. "I wanted you to know first!"

"Calm down girl. I'm happy to hear you made it. I'm kinda busy so I'll call you later," Kim replied in a very nonchalant tone.

"Alright…I'll talk to you later," Stacy said hanging up.

The news traveled fast but Kim didn't want to hear it. The fact that Stacy had her life on track and was leaving her behind upset her deep down inside. She sat back and compared their lives and though she had the same options as Stacy somewhere she had gone left. Stacy was on her way to one of best colleges and she was going to still be in the hood with some fake ass ballers. Only if she would have stayed focused and followed Stacy then maybe she wouldn't feel left behind or out.

Stacy answered her phone when she saw Joey calling her. "Hey baby, I know it's loud in the background but I wanted to call you personally and tell you how proud I am of you," Joey yelled over the deep bass.

"Thanks Boo. I called Kim to tell her and she was acting all funny and stuff," Stacy said still thrown off by Kim's attitude.

"Don't worry about that. You are her girl, she is probably tripping because she is going to miss you."

"I guess," she sighed. I'll catch you later. Be careful and tell Rome I said Hi."

The next few weeks before graduation flew by lightning fast. Mrs. Moore had bought Stacy a beautiful gown and a new art set as her presents. She looked so beautiful the morning of graduation that her mother made sure to capture the moment by taking dozens of pictures.

J-Rock looked charming in his 3 piece suit that matched her gown. When he saw Stacy walking up, he had to catch his breath. She was absolutely gorgeous.

The ceremony was nice and Stacy received a loud round of applause and a standing ovation from her mom and J-Rock when her name was called. After the ceremony Kim joined them at dinner at her favorite restaurant.

The summer months were filled with the anticipation of what Stacy's new move would bring. J-Rock had bought her a Honda Civic as his graduation gift so she could get around the city. He had accompanied that gift with a promise ring so she knew just how strong his commitment was to her. They spent almost every free moment together.

J-Rock's plans were coming together. He had save $120,000 to invest in buying foreclosed homes around the city. He had taken a 40 hour real estate course and was well versed on the ins and outs of the industry.

Stacy had designed his company logo and business cards for him to complete the look of professionalism. With Rondo by his side as a loyal friend and partner, they set their goals even higher while Stacy would be away.

The night before she left, J-Rock set up a family night at Dave & Buster's for both of their families and their friends.

"Thank you Joey for everything thing. I really appreciate all that you have done for me. I just hope that you will be good while I'm gone," Stacy said as they leaned against the counter waiting for more tickets.

"Chill out Lil' Ma, I got you. I'mma hold shit down here so when you through, you can come home to a full plate. I'll be coming to see you and we'll talk every day, I promise," he said while hugging her waist.

"I'm gonna miss you so much, Baby. We gotta work through this and I'm going to have Kim put a GPS on your ass," she joked.

"You soooo funny," he said sarcastically. "Come on, it's getting late you have an early flight to catch. Oh, I'll be bringing your car up to you next with Rondo and Rook."

She gave him a quick kiss and smiled. "I love you Joey."

"I love you too, Stacy."

The next morning her mother took her to the airport to send her off to explore a new way of life. Though Detroit was a big city, New York was a different animal.

They prayed for a safe flight and her mom assured her that she loved her with everything and that she was so proud of her accomplishments. Stacy hugged her mom and headed into the departure doors. Once seated on her flight, she looked out the window and said, "Next stop is the big city of dreams."

CHAPTER EIGHT

When Stacey landed in New York, she headed straight for her dorm to settle in and to call her mom and Joey. The city was nice and calm compared to the traffic per square inch in New York. Here, people raced up and down the crowded streets rushing to get to work or school. The buildings were huge and large advertisements were splattered everywhere, just like in the movies. She loved the campus and figured once her car arrived she would be ok.

Joey had given her $10,000 to put in the bank to hold her over until later. She had six classes to prepare for while still dedicating time to her art schedule. School was much harder than she expected but she stayed focused and looked to finish in three years.

J-Rock kept all his promises by bringing her car and they continued to talked every day. He stayed loyal to her and never missed a phone call or left a text unanswered. Meanwhile his business was picking up and money was rolling in fast.

The Fenkell Boys were all about the cash and J-Rock's dad enjoyed watching his two boys run the family business.

Over the years Stacy never got lonely or questioned her relationship with Joey. Maybe because Kim played a major role in that because she kept her informed of any street gossip and kept a watchful eye on him,

In her last year in New York, things suddenly took a turn for the worse. Though her school work was going well and her degree was basically in the bag, shit had home had gotten off track and no one would tell her why or how. She could tell something was different with Joey and Kim's attitude but she couldn't figure out why.

Then one night after a party at Club Legend's, J-Rock was about to leave the club late. To his surprise Kim had been there with her girls and had a little too much to drink. A squabble had almost taken place between some girls from the West Warren area and the girls from

Bright'mo. Since J-Rock had pull and respect he was able to stop the drama.

Kim was upset and drunk so J-Rock forced her into his new Audi 8 and demanded that she let him take her home. In the car Kim cried as they drove to her house.

"Thanks J, for helping me out back there," she said.

"Man, you my girl's best friend and I'm not gonna let something happen to you. But, you gotta chill shorty with all that extra shit," he said staring straight ahead at the road.

"I know, I know. I miss my girl and can't wait until she gets back home.

"Yeah, I miss her too. Now tell me where you want to go."

"To my crib on Log Cabin," she said.

When they finally pulled up on her block she was knocked out sleep. J-Rock woke her up to let her know she was home. She roused a bit then shot up, opening the door to throw up on the curb. J-Rock rushed to the other side to help her out the car, praying that she hadn't vomited inside his car.

"I'm so sorry J-Rock. I'm fucked up though, I need you to help into the house."

"I gotcha drunk ass. Where the keys at?" he asked laughing.

He helped her get to the porch and got the keys out of her purse to open the door. When they got inside she asked him to wait around until she checked out the house. While he waited he looked at some pictures she had on her mantle. Some included Stacy smiling back at him looking cute. When he heard Kim come back in the room he was surprised to see her standing there all cleaned up with just her bra and panties on.

"Yeah, you like what you see don't you?" she asked rubbing her hands down her body across her breast and landing on her covered pussy.

"Man, you tripping girl," he said not able to take his eyes off of what was standing in front of him.

Come here, Joey. I ain't gone bite or tell on you, nigga," she replied in her sexy voice.

"Girl, you fooling! I'm out," he said walking to the door.

She ran in front of him and locked the front door and put the key in her bra. Then she laid on the couch, grabbing Joey shirt so he had to sit down next to her. She laid back and opened her legs to let him see her pussy. With her panties pulled over to the side she started playing with it encouraging J-Rock to join in.

"Umm, look at this pretty pussy boy. Ain't she pretty and wet? I been waiting to fuck you for so long Joey," she said while grabbing his hand.

He knew he was in a tight position. He had always known she'd had a crush on him but never thought she would take it to this extreme level. He felt the front of his pants tightening in the front as he fought off the hard on that was steadily growing. She was hard to resist. He calmly loosened her bra and grabbed her nice sized breast as the keys fell out on to the couch. He grabbed then as her eyes were closed as she intently pleasured herself.

Once she put her fingers into her pussy and motioned to for him to enter her, he jumped up and ran to unlock the door.

"Man, you are my girl's best friend. We can't play her like this, babe. You drunk shorty, get yourself together. I'm out," he said closing the door.

He could hear her screaming his name and telling him to come back on the other side of the door, as she angrily threw her pump at the door in frustration.

It was already three a.m. so he rushed home. Once in bed he texted Stacy:

:Hey Boo, love and miss you. Can't wait until you get home. Call me when you get up. Xoxoxoxoxo:

After sending the text he relaxed and thought to himself, "Ole girl crazy as hell. I did the right thang and the next best thang to do is keep it to myself. It will only cause problems coming from me, so I'll let Kim tell her during girl talk or whatever."

The next morning he awoke to a text from Stacy:

:Hey baby. I'm on my way to class. Thanks for texting but ya ass should have been home before 3 am. Be good and stay out of trouble. I'm watching you lol. See ya in 3 weeks. We did it! Xoxoxoxoxo Love Stacy:

He couldn't believe that three years had flown by. IT seemed like yesterday that he had sent her off. He was just as excited as he was for her to be back in his life permanently.

While she was away he had stacked up to a quarter million in profits from the J&S Real Estate Company. He had recently purchased a 3000 square foot home in Garden city. It was four bedrooms with two and a half baths. When she got home he would surprise her with all that she needed to be happy. He'd had the basement reconstructed into an art studio with all the top of the line equipment and supplies. He had left the walls a blank canvas so she could decorate them with her own art.

Even if she chose to stay at home with her mom she would have a key and a home with him. He had three weeks to plan for her arrival and surprise party.

Rondo helped with renting the hall and arranging for all the invites to be mailed. Kim hadn't contacted him since that crazy night but he knew she had been in touch with Stacy.

After several weeks of hard work and planning it was almost time to take their love to another level. Until then, they continued to talk and text, inspiring each other to love and learn in the future.

CHAPTER NINE

"Surprise!" everyone yelled when Stacy and J-Rock walked into the building. When she had pulled in from the long drive, J-Rock had met up with her and said he needed to make a stop at a commercial property. She had no clue that he had planned a party and was completely caught off guard.

She was totally shocked as she opened her eyes to see all her family and friends dressed in party attire. Some of her old friends from the neighborhood were there and even some of her new friends from college. She couldn't believe it as she walked through the crowd.

As she walked through speaking to everyone out of nowhere comes a loud boisterous scream, "Hey BFF!!" Kim shouted over the loud music system.

"Hey girl! You looking cute as usual," Stacy stood back and said.

"You too! I missed you so much. Let's toast to you," Kim said raising her glass.

J-Rock was standing next to Stacy feeling kinda awkward. This was the first time that he had seen Kim since her failed seduction attempt. Neither of them knew if the other had told Stacy what had happened. So to avoid any suspicion he calmly kissed Stacy on the cheek and excused himself to allow them to catch up.

He was excited to have his wifey back and couldn't wait to spend some time alone with her. He was happy to have the support of her mother, who sat in the VIP section and watched the partygoers. It meant a lot to Stacy so it meant a lot to him.

Once things died down and everyone was full and drunk, they sat around and talked about her plans for the future. She planned to stay at home with her mother until the time was right with Joey. She had no idea how he was living or his plans for them as a couple.

"Excuse me. May I have your attention please," he said into the mic that the DJ handed him. He was standing on the stage about to make a toast to the love of his life. "I would like to thank everyone for coming out and supporting this wonderful event. Stacy has come a long way and went through so much to achieve her goals in life. It's an honor to be a part of her life and to witness her success. I would like to wish her all the blessings she deserves and again, thank you to all her true friends and family for supporting her," he ended while raising his champagne glass.

Stacy stood up and smiled as she and her mother raised their glasses to celebrate. Several hours later the crowd started to slowly leave. Stacy wanted to spend the night with Joey, but first she needed to talk to Kim alone.

She saw Kim posted at the bar so she headed over to her, "Hey BFF, let's talk," she said saddling up next to her.

"It's hot in here, let's step outside and get some air," Kim suggested. They walked over and leaned against J-Rock's car.

"So how have you been Kim? It seems like you've been avoiding me all night. Is everything ok?" Stacy stated.

"Nahh, Boo, it's not like that at all. I was just trying not to take the spotlight from you or ruin anything. You know I act a fool when that liquor get in my system," she joked.

"Well I'm home now girl, so you straight. How as my man since I've been gone? Anything new I need to know?" she asked again.

Kim was thrown off balance by the questions, so she simply shook her head no and smiled. She thought to herself, "Was this the time to tell her about her actions or did Joey's scary ass beat her to the punch?"

"Well it's late as hell and I already know you need to get your groove back, Stella," Kim joked.

"Hell yeah, it's show time baby!" Stacy said. "Plus you see how sexy my nigga looking," she said licking her lips.

"Well enjoy your night, girl. I'll call you tomorrow to catch up and hang out," Kim suggested.

"Alright be safe. I'll check in with you in the pm," Stacy said.

J-Rock and Rondo were ready to leave as they walked up to the car. "What up baby? You staying with me tonight or what?" J-Rock joked giving Stacy a kiss.

"Boy shut up. You already know what time it is," she responded rolling her eyes at her lover.

Kim made her exit she slyly took another glance back at the happy couple as she walked away.

Rondo was watching her from a distance and noticed the strange look she had given them. He walked up to the J-Rock and Stacy to say his good-byes. "Alright my nigga, I see you are in good hands so I'm gon leave ya'll alone for the night. I'm gon head to the studio to hook up with Pone. See ya Stacy, it's really good to have you back," he said while throwing up the peace sign and walking away to his Porsche truck.

They hopped inside the all-white, Audi 8 and headed for J-Rock's newly purchased home in Garden City. When they arrived Stacy looked on in amazement.

"Joey this is so nice. I love the landscaping and area. Why didn't you tell me you got a house?" she asked curious.

"I wanted it to be a surprise, and I also wanted you to be proud of me."

"I'm already proud of you. You know I got your back baby," she said.

"Let's go inside so I can show you around."

They entered through the two car garage and headed into the house through the side door. Joey disarmed the alarm system and then armed it again once they were in the house.

"Oh, my God Joey! This house is huge! You did a great job!

"Thank you, but there's more," he said.

He proceeded to show her around the house ending his tour in the finished basement.

"Oh! Shit!" she yelled when he turned the lights on in the basement and saw the specially designed office and art studio that he'd had built for her.

Tears filled her eyes as he sat on the stairs watching her glow.

"This is all for you baby. I wanted to show you how much I love and support your dreams."

Stacy stood there speechless as she took it all in. She ran and hugged him and kissed his face,

"Since you've been gone, my business has picked up enough so that my street life is limited. I've saved over a quarter of a million and bought this house with cash. I'm 22 now and I want out of the life," he said with a pause. He stood up and led Stacy upstairs to the master bedroom.

When he opened the door her face lit up with joy. There was a table set up with a bottle of Moet and two glasses in an ice bucket. Rose petals were scattered about the room and there was an envelope on the bed.

"This is for you baby."

She took the letter still trying to take it all in.

He continued, "You know I ain't the kind of guy to beat around the bush. Time is the only thing that we can't get back," he said.

She opened the envelope and inside were a set of keys to the house and the alarm code. Also inside was fifty thousand dollars and the paperwork to start her LLC.

"This is some money to help you start up your own art business and a little bit to go shopping with."

She cried into this shoulder as she hugged him, "Boo, I don't know what to say or how to start to thank you!"

"Oh, you'll do just fine. I told you I had your back and all I need to be complete is you," he said softly while reaching into his pocket. "Baby, I know it's late but I can't wait any longer. I want you to move in with me and let me take care of you. Not just for a while but for the rest of your life."

He pulled from his pocket a three karat diamond ring and kneeled to one knee. He was finally ready to ask the most important question of his life.

Stacy screamed when she saw the ring, "Oh shit, Joey!! Stop playing! Are you serious?"

"Yes, all I want to know is will you marry me?" he asked.

"Hell yes!!" she screamed as he placed the ring on her finger, then stood up to embrace his new fiancé.

Minutes later they were toasting to each other then headed to the bed to engage in a passionate love making session. After several hours of catching up they fell asleep in each other's arms until morning.

The next day Stacy woke up only to find Joey already up and out. He had left a note on the fridge that read:

Sorry I tried to wake you but you were sound asleep. Rondo and I had to check out some properties before the City County Building got to crowded. I'll catch you later or text me when you get up. Until later, love your fiancé.

She got up and made a small breakfast then called her mother to tell her the news. Her mother was thrilled to hear that her only daughter would be marrying a man that seemed to truly love her. He had asked for her blessings months before and she was happy that he had decided to ask the big question.

"Yeah, and he gave me keys to the house so I think I am going to stay over here," Stacy said.

"Well your room is always open, if you need it honey," Mrs. Moore responded. She figured it was coming any way so she accepted the fact that her baby was all grown up.

"Thanks Ma, I'll let you finish work and I'll be over later. I have to call Kim and tell her the news."

Kim had been at the nail shop for several hours when Stacy called. She had been trying to grab some of the walk in clients. She answered the phone, "Hey BFF. I'm really happy to have you back."

"What's up Sis? I have to tell you about last night. Do you have a minute?" she asked excited.

"I tell you what, I'm over booked right now so let's do lunch then we can talk."

"Cool, I'll come pick you up at 11:30 then we can head over to Friday's in Dearborn. You still at Rome's shop on Joy Rd?"

"Yeah, I'll see you at 11:30 girl," Kim said and ended the conversation.

Since she had an hour to kill she decided to text Joey and headed down in the basement to organize her art studio. All kinds of ideas were in her head as she sketched a logo for her company. Her plan was to invest thirty of the fifty thousand into her business. The rest she would go shopping and save.

She sat the pencil down and looked at the name she had come up with, "Unique Creations." This business would create revenue by designing logos for businesses and selling and purchasing fine arts and crafts. Of course most of her own work would be showcased.

Finally after several minutes of thinking, her cellphone rang with a call from Joey.

"Hey Boo, you finally up huh?" he asked.

"Yeah about to go have lunch with Kim to catch up on the gossip and hood news," she laughed.

He tensed up at that news but said, "Well, I'll be home around dinner time. I have to drive up to Flint to pick up a few contract permits."

"I'll be done cooking around 7:30 and I'll pick up a movie too," she said happily into the phone.

"Cool. I'll catch up with you later. I love you."

"I love you too, Joey."

She hung up the phone then rushed to get dressed to meet up with Kim. She set the alarm before she left and drove into the city to pick up her girl. She couldn't wait to show off her ring.

Kim was already sitting outside the shop when she pulled up. "Hop in girl! You ready?" she asked.

"Hell yeah. I'm starving," Kim said relaxing in the passenger seat,

On the way to the restaurant they laughed and joked like old times. Stacy explained to Kim how she wanted to open her own business in the next few weeks to help Joey out.

"That's a good idea for real girl. I'll be down to help you any way you need me too," Kim offered.

"Thanks, Boo. I'm going to need all the help I can get. I want to do it right the first time."

They ordered a few drinks and looked at the menu after they were seated. Stacy could no longer contain herself as she said, "So let me tell you all about last night."

"I'm all ears cause I know it went down something serious," said Kim. "Start talking!"

After hearing all the details about the house, money and awesome sex Kim was all in. Stacy saved the best part for last, "He asked me to marry him! I got engaged!" she said showing off the huge rock on her left hand.

"I knew something was up. You can't help but notice that big ass thang on your hand, especially when you were driving. But I thought it was a promise ring," Kim said with the slightest bit of shade.

"Naw baby, he got down on one knee and he had even asked for my mom's blessings," Stacy said.

"Well congratulations Boo. I hope ya'll make it work. But do you think you guys are ready for this? You are only twenty one and you've only been home for two days."

Stacy was a little thrown off by Kim's response. She had congratulated her but then questioned her decision.

She was feeling some negative coming from Kim and couldn't figure out why.

"Yeah Kim, I'm ready. Joey has held me down for years and now it's my turn to the same for him, but for life."

They continued to eat and talk for a little while before heading back towards the shop. They joked about Rondo still being crazy and listened to Aaliyah's new cd.

"Ok girl, thanks for lunch," Kim said as she exited the car.

"I'm about to hit the mall. I'll text you later," Stacy said before she rolled the window up. She had a few hours to kill before she and Joey would be hooking up so she headed to Somerset Mall. She went on a true blue shopping spree and still made it home in time to cook dinner.

Joey walked in to a full course meal and his beautiful fiancé sitting at the table. After dinner they watched, "Dead Presidents," the movie Stacy had picked up.

Joey never liked talking about his street life or business with anyone, so this allowed for very little dialogue. She filled the conversation with her own business ideas and of course he said supported her 100 percent.

But for some reason, Stacy got that same feeling she had experienced earlier that day with Kim. She ignored it like earlier and continued to think positively. She was home now and in due time, things would reveal themselves...

CHAPTER TEN

After several months of living together as an engaged couple, things were still a little out of whack. With Joey running his business twenty four hours and staying committed to his crew, his time at home was rare yet much needed. Stacy was in the process of getting her companies first clients but still craved Joey's undivided attention.

A lot of nights she would spend worrying about Joey and thinking the worst. She always assumed he was living a double life, but could never prove it. It just didn't seem right that he would spend that much time away from the house. She wanted to trust him, especially since he came home every night and left his cell phone out in plain view.

She had figured in her mind that while she away at school, he had been involved in another relationship being that all men needed sex on demand. Kim hadn't told her about anything unordinary, but again she could be playing the neutral role to avoid conflict.

Stacy felt like it was time to do a little more research to prove her theory. Whenever Joey would come home she would smell him and his boxers for traces of soap or perfume.

Sometimes she would engaged in sex just to see if she stayed hard or came strongly as usual. Several times when he would be out in the streets she would have a friend approach to flirt or she would follow him to different locations.

At one point it got to the level that she wanted to contact "Cheaters" to pursue her assumption. It was difficult trying to pin point his actions cause of his lifestyle. She figured in her mind that if she wasn't getting his full attention, then someone else was.

He never gave in to the arguments or allegations, he just continued to stay focus on his money and his brand. Stacy had it all and was too blind to realize it. Spending so much time looking for dirt on him allowed her to become a product of her own insecurities. Joey was a good man and only out to structure his life so that they both could benefit in the future.

He placed everything at her footsteps but yet she still wanted more. Stacy yearned for that feeling she felt the day they first met. She had to get to the bottom of this and she knew actually how and who to go see. After playing inspector gadget, she picked up the phone and called Kim.

"Hey Stacy, what up girl?" she answered.

"Shit, at the house chilling. I was wondering if you wanted to come by and have a drink with me. Plus I can show you the flyers that I printed up for you to display at the shop," she requested.

"Cool I get off at nine so I'll fall thru after that. J-rock cool with me stopping by?" she asked curious.

"Girl yeah, he already know you my dog and he okay with it. Anyhow he'll be gone until late, they got some type of seminar they going to. So fall through after work, I even made two sweet potatoes pies," she stated.

"Oh shit! That's my favorite! Alright catch you later then, "Kim said before hanging up.

Kim had been around Stacy every day and knew about all the speculations that she had about J-rock. She just figured that as long as the attention was on other hoes then she would be safe. Kim, knew that if she found out about the night of the party. That would ruin their friendship forever and cause conflict in the house as well. Since so much time had gone by she felt strongly that J-rock hadn't told Stacy, cause it never came up.

Deep inside she still wanted J-rock and needed Stacy to drop the ball, so that she could try and pick it up. She vowed to secretly destroy their relationship to get to the heart of J-rock.

Later that night Kim arrived at the house in Garden City. Stacy let her in for the first time and showed her around.

"Damn girl, this layout is very nice. I love it," Kim said looking around with envy in her heart.

"Yeah can you believe he did this all by himself?" Stacy replied.

"He know his shit. What is this granite or marble?" Kim asked.

"Yeah girl that's the real shit. Let me show you my art studio," Stacy demanded.

As they walked to the basement, Kim observed every inch of the luxurious home, wishing it was hers. "Girl this shit nice as hell."

"Thanks have a seat, I need to talk to you for a minute," Stacy demanded.

"What's on ya mind Boo?" Kim asked nervously.

All that she could think of was, "Damn, she know about the crazy situation."

"You already know me and how I feel about my baby," Stacy started.

"True that."

"Well, the last few weeks things have been kinda at a standstill. He's been busy all the time and tired when he comes home. I think there is someone else and he is living a double life. Be real with me Kim, how was he when I was gone?" Stacy asked with a pleading look on her face.

Kim took a drink from her glass to calm her nerves and said, "Listen Stacy, I don't know all of his actions. Rondo never talks about what they do, plus he is just a man Stacy." She was relieved again that Stacy's concerns had nothing to do with her.

"I know, I know but something ain't right girl. I can feel him slipping away and I know business is not more important than me," she said sadly.

Now that Kim had seen an emotional weakness, she shot her move to create some drama. "Ok, now listen. I got this friend who nails I've been doing for a few summers. She said she knows J-Rock from the hood and she knows someone who use to fuck him."

"Who the fuck is she?" Stacy interrupted.

"Wait, Wait! Let me finish before you go all Vivica Fox on me," said Kim. "She saw J-Rock at Rome's shop and pointed me out. She claimed that he was fucking her sister named Christine from Southfield," she finished.

"Do you think it's true? In fact, can you put me in touch with this bitch, Kim? I'm about to marry this nigga and I need to know that I am doing the right thing," she said angrily.

Moments later they heard the alarm to the house being disarmed. J-Rock and Rondo walked in looking for the girls. They knew Kim was over because they saw her Impala in the driveway.

J-Rock headed to put his profits away in the safe as the girls walked into the kitchen to greet them. Stacy was upset but she tried not to let it show. She didn't want to give up her secret yet. "Hey Rondo."

"What up doe, Stacy and Little Kim," Rondo joked.

"Where's Joey," Stacy said through a smile.

"Oh, he went upstairs. Tell him I'll catch him later in the hood. My cell banging with missed calls," he said noticing her strange energy. He looked down at his phone and started walking out.

"Yeah, girl. I'm gon bounce too. I'll call you tonight to check on you, "Kim hugged her as she departed.

While walking out of the house, Rondo and Kim looked at each other trying to detect the awkward energy in the room.

Joey walked downstairs and noticed that everyone was gone. Stacy had poured a glass of Moet and orange juice and sat on the bar stool awaiting his return.

"Hey baby, I missed you today," he said reaching in for a hug.

Without warning, Stacy threw the champagne in his face, causing him to step back. "What the fuck is wrong wit you?"

Stacy charged at him full speed, screaming, "You mother fucker! I've been loyal to your black ass and this is what I get in return?"

"Dig, you better calm the fuck down and stop putting your hands on me," he shouted trying to stop her blows.

Stacy wouldn't stop bucking as she kicked off the wall which forced Joey to fall backwards, landing on the round glass table. He sat there for a minute looking dazed and confused with broken glass all around him. Quickly got up and chased after her, only to find her in the living room looking for his stashed gun!

"What the fuck is going on?" he asked grabbing her by the neck.

"You cheating Bitch! I hate you! Why couldn't you just be honest?" she shouted still trying to fight him.

He threw her up against the wall still choking her. She scratched at his hands and gasped for air until he released her.

"So now you gon choke me because you fucked up huh?" she said allowing the air to fill her lungs.

Anger flowed all through his body. "Listen I'm gon tell your stupid ass one more time. I haven't cheated on you with no fucking body!" He watched her cry and continued, "Whatever information you got is completely fucking wrong!"

"You better clean your fucking trail, mother fucker!" she yelled.

"Man, I'm out. Clean this shit up, stupid ass. And get ya fucking facts straight," he demanded before he stormed out of the house.

Joey got in the car and called Rondo. He told him to meet him at Club 747 in Inkster to help him figure this shit out. As he sat in the parking lot waiting on Rondo to pull up he turned his cellphone off to avoid any more arguing.

Once Rondo arrived they sat in the club and enjoyed the dancers as they entertained them for loose bills.

"Man! She tripped on you like that dawg?" Rondo asked shocked to hear the news.

"Hell yeah! Man she lucky a nigga love her crazy ass because she was almost outta there!" J-Rock said.

After a few dances and a few drinks Rondo said," Dawg, you think Kim's hating ass told her some shit? I mean she was looking shady as hell earlier at the house."

"I don't know, man. They was together earlier today and then she was gone when I came back downstairs," J-rock said, replaying the events in his mind and thinking about Kim's hating ways. He wondered if Kim had told the story about the incident and flipped the script on him, but Stacy hadn't mentioned any names in her crazy tirade.

He didn't know what the hell was going on. He leaned back in his chair and took in all the stripper glory that was in front of him and decided to take care of his personal shit later. He and Rondo ordered another bottle and chilled.

Back at the house after cleaning up the mess that they had made, Stacy called Kim to tell her what had happened and as surprised at her reaction.

"You shouldn't have even brought it up," Kim had said with not a bit of sympathy or emotion.

Stacy wasn't sure what Kim had thought she would do with the information but now that she had used it, Kim acted like it was her fault that J-Rock had cheated. She was too tired to argue so she ended the conversation and got in the bed.

It was 2:15 when J-Rock pulled in to the driveway. He noticed the bedroom light was still on. He didn't want to argue or fight anymore. He was innocent and he knew this, but how was he supposed to prove that to Stacy if he didn't know what or who the hell she was talking about?

Stacy laid there half asleep waiting for him to come home. She also secretly wanted to make sure he didn't smell like pussy.

They spoke for a brief second while he tried to explain himself. Once he heard the name of the female but not the source, he flipped.

"Christina who? Baby I never fucked with her or no other hoe while you were gone. Yes I know who you are talking about but that's it," he said sitting up in the bed.

Since it was late and she had no concrete proof, she let it slide until later. Now it was time to test his manhood to see if had run to another woman, over the past few hours. She allowed herself to be seduced by his charm that led to make up sex.

Minutes later she made him cum on her tongue just to check the velocity of his ejaculation. She could always tell if he was extra happy to get some by the color, texture and amount of cum his body produced. After sex they slept, both with one eye open, afraid of the others potential actions.

Over the next few months thing slowly went back to normal. There was still some tension but for the most part they were ok. He kept up his business and hustle routine while she started her company and watched his every move.

Kim and Rondo had been around as counselors and friends but neither would trust the other's advice. Stacy had spent more time with Kim than J-Rock and this gave Kim just enough room to manipulate the situation even more.

Kim was wild and lived the single life to the fullest. She had several men in her life and no direction where to go or be taken. J-Rock started to notice a different Stacy and began to show more attention to seal the void. He would come home early, bring flowers and try to engage in conversations more. He felt slightly rejected only because in the back of her mind she still though he was cheating.

LOVE AND BETRAYAL

Stacy started staying out late, talking back and seemed to take on a lot of Kim's unruly traits. Even though J-Rock didn't like the new Stacy, he still remained loyal and dedicated to only her. He always said that it was only a phase she was going through and she would outgrow it soon.

Months turned into seasons and seasons turned into a few years. Their relationship wasn't dead but it wasn't growing either. As long as Kim had control and a voice, it would only be a matter of time before another woman's trash would be another woman's treasure.

CHAPTER ELEVEN

Stacy had been home for a few years now and things were still in motion. Her business was picking up and her relationship with Joey was stagnated. Ever so often she would visit Mrs. Moore for advice about certain things, but her mom would never offer any.

Kim was still single and her BFF to the end. Whenever Stacy needed to get away or vent, Kim was always available. They had taken trips to Mexico and Vegas over the summers without Joey and Rondo. This had allowed Kim to really push the envelope to see how Stacy reacted away from home.

Kim knew that she was unstable and uncertain about her relationship, but she wasn't quite ready to let him go. Kim needed another plan to increase the tension.

She wanted Joey to herself and would stop at nothing to get him.

Back at the home front, J-Rock was still aware of the lack of attention he displayed sometimes and tried to work on it. Between running his company and the Fenkell Boys Organization, time and money was a necessity. He didn't want to lose his fiancé and he didn't want to smother her either. Their communication level was mid-level and he searched for advice from his mom on how to make things work.

J-Rock's family was supportive of their engagement and felt as if Stacy was not a gold digger. All the advice they gave helped keep him strong enough to deal with the neglect and false accusations.

During the course of the summer of 2003 both Stacy and Joey were on their way to fame and fortune. Whenever seen together they were known as the power couple and everyone loved to be around them. Throughout time they shared a lot of good times but Joey just felt deep inside that something was missing.

So he began to stay alert and hired Rondo to do a little investigating. Their wedding plans were springing into action and before the big leap he needed confirmation on every step that she took.

Meanwhile it was 85 degrees outside and all through the city people scrambled like eggs to find excitement. Every club and park was filled to the max with party people enjoying the good weather. Car systems blasted, "Cash Money Records, T.I and Rockbottom's latest cd's. The Bosses were sporting Cartier frames, Gator gym shoes or Cole Haan's for comfort, and their automobiles rode on 22 or 24 inch rims to show the owner had status.

J-Rock had bought Stacy a 2003 Infiniti with 22 inch rims as a birthday present along with a $20,000 four karat Omega Chain and Heart charm. J-Rock had made over a half a million in two years and was celebrating by upgrading everything around him.

He gave Rondo his Audi 8 and bought himself an all-white BMW 745 with 22 inch Ashanti rims. On his wrist he wore a $25,000 Piquet with matching bracelet. They were both on top of their game and trying to reach the stars.

Stacy has arranged to have a showcase for her company at Cobo Hall for a selected few from around the globe. Displaying her artwork and other special pieces would bring her more money and more clientele. She took pride in her craft and business sense alike. The gathering would feature expensive Art Deco and Tiffany collectibles.

The night of the showcase Joey and her arrived as a team to meet and greet the guest. After several minutes of mingling, J-Rock headed to the second floor to chill. He didn't want to crowd her or take any attention off the guest of honor, so he admired from a distance her body of work.

Shortly after the doors opened her friends began to arrive. Everyone was dressed in their finest after five ensembles, even Kim who arrived with two handsome men.

Once Stacy spotted Kim she made her way over quickly to greet her.

"Hey girlfriend, you look nice," Kim said looking her up and down.

"Look at you, girl! All dressed up like a baby doll," Stacy said giving her a hug.

"I like the set up Stacy, this is really nice."

"Thank you. Not too bad for my first showcase, huh?"

"Well where is the man of the event," Kim asked looking around.

"You know he's upstairs, trying let me bask in the moment."

"That's cool. We as you can see I brought a few gentlemen with me that love to spend money," Kim said jokingly to Stacy.

"I noticed. How are you two doing? My name is Stacy and I am the host of this Art Show," she explained while extending her hand for a handshake.

The two nice looking men were well-dressed and smelled very nice. One was short with muscles covering every inch of his body. He had long braided hair and a full beard. The other was tall, brown skinned with short curly hair and a smile as radiant as the sun. They reminded Stacy of Larenz Tate and Tyson Beckford.

"Hello, my name is Ricky and this is my boy Terrance or Big-T for short," the short dude said.

"Well it's nice to meet you both. Any friend of Kim's is a friend of mine. Let me show you around the gallery," she smiled and suggested.

She took them on a tour of the each exhibit describing each piece in detail. As the men examined one of the pieces Kim whispered, "These are my boys from Miami and they are down there making moves. They are giving a party at Captain's on Saturday, you should go with me."

"I'll let you know, girl," Stacy replied with a slight grin.

The group stopped in front of a piece that caught Terrance's eye. It was a statue of a man with a woman holding him from behind, crying. Stacy stepped forward to explain it, "I call this piece "Strength," because behind every black man is a strong black woman."

"I love it. I'll take this one, sexy," Terrance requested.

"Don't you want to at least know how much it is?" she asked laughing.

"Doesn't matter. I know beauty ain't cheap, so however much it is, I'm willing to pay it," he responded.

"It's $13,000 and I can wrap it and ship for you if you'd like," Stacy said.

He pulled his credit card out of his wallet and Stacy motioned to the sales clerk to bring a purchase order form and hand held credit card machine. She tagged the statue as sold and thanked the gentleman, 'Thank you, Terrance. I'm really grateful."

"You can ship it to my condo in Miami. I'll be there tomorrow and I'll be flying back for the party. I hope to see you there," he said taking his receipt.

"I'd be happy to come. Now if you gentlemen would excuse us for a moment," she said grabbing Kim's arm and heading to the bathroom.

Kim stood in the mirror refreshing her lipstick while Stacy leaned up against the sink.

"So spill it," she said to Kim.

"Look, them niggas fine as hell and they got money to burn," Kim said, smacking her lips.

"They cute girl, but you know I ain't fucking around on Joey's ass," Stacy replied.

"I know bitch, Dang! I'm just saying come to the party and show your support. The nigga just cashed out 13 grand," Kim reminded her.

"What kind of work do they do?" she asked just curious.

"They real street niggas and they got the entire east side on lock down with they shit. They connected Boo, trust me, we good," Kim said with confidence.

"Ok, I'm in. Call me later," Stacy said as they exited the bathroom to meet back up with the boys.

While walking back their way Stacy noticed J-Rock and Rondo pointing at the two dudes. So she detoured and told Kim that she would call her later.

Kim chatted for a few minutes with the guys then they made their way to the exit. In her mind she knew that she had planted another seed in her feeble minded friends head. All the time that Stacy had been giving her guided tour, she hadn't once thought to see where J-Rock was. Kim had already peeped him and Rondo standing in the balcony watching their every move.

J-Rock hadn't really thought twice about the guys or the purchase that he had made but he made a mental note to have Rondo to do a check up on the outsiders they had met earlier in traffic.

The showcase was a success and Stacy had grossed $60,000 from the lavish event. That night she and Joey had a wonderful time at home having sex and feeding each other desserts.

Both of their minds were clear from drama and they enjoyed the night as a power couple. A few days had gone by and Stacy had gotten a call from Kim asking about the party. She had agreed to go and kept her word to Kim as a friend.

That Saturday night they hooked up and rode together in Stacy's new Infiniti. They pulled up and valet parked outside the crowded club. The line was two blocks long as party goers jockeyed for position according to status.

Once they stepped up on the sidewalk, they walked past the crowd to talk to the security guards by the door.

"Hello ladies," the big guy spoke with the Visper security shirt.

"Hey honey, could you page Ricky or Big-T for me please?" asked Kim.

"Sure thang, sexy," he replied looking them both up and down.

Moments later Big-T appeared at the door wearing a nice suit without the jacket and a pair of Big Block Gator Boots. His whole body glowed with excessive diamonds on his wrist, arm, neck, ears and glasses. He looked like million bucks as he told the guard to let them thru.

The inside was packed from wall to wall as the DJ played all the latest songs fast and slow. They headed to VIP section where Ricky was sitting with three bottles of Don P and Red Bull Energy drinks.

"Well, ain't this a nice look," Ricky said over the loud system.

"Hey, honey! You looking good!" Kim shouted as she gave them both hugs gently. "Ya'll remember my girl, Stacy, right?" she shouted over the music.

"How could we forget a face so beautiful and body like a Coke bottle? Plus she talked me out of thirteen racks," joked Big-T.

"Hey, ya'll. Nice party," Stacy said with a smile. 'Thanks for inviting me."

The party was jumping, but Stacy had solely come to show her gratitude to Big-T for supporting her. Unbeknownst to her, this was a blind date requested by

Big-T and orchestrated by Kim. If Stacy showed any sign of weakness, then that would allow her to gain major ground on her mission to destroy.

Both ladies were looking fly. Kim in her one piece by Louis Vuitton and a pair of six inch Red Bottoms to match. While Stacy was dressed in a two piece Christian Dior skirt set with a classic pair of black Gucci pumps. They both wore Chanel earrings and bracelets to match.

The men invited them over to the VIP area to have a few drinks. They were drinking a drink called the "Mask." This was a drink from Miami they had come up with to give you the ultimate buzz. It was a Red Bull and Dom P with a slice of lemon. The four then engaged in drinks and conversation until the late hours. Stacy thought about J-Rock a time or two, but she had made sure he had plans to ensure that she didn't bump into him.

The party was drama free which made it a success in Stacy's book. After the club let out, the four stayed behind to help total the profits and chill a little longer. Kim noticed that Big-T and Stacy were getting better acquainted, so she quietly kept her eye on the pair.

Since it was getting late the men asked the ladies if it was ok for them to walk them to their car before they left for the after party at CCC's. The girls agreed but declined the offer to go to the after party. They chatted briefly at the car before saying their goodbyes.

As Kim and Ricky joked together, Big-T slipped Stacy his business card.

"I had a wonderful time entertaining you tonight. Here is my number, whenever your man makes you mad, feel free to give me a call," he said.

Stacy had been through a lot over the last few years and to some degree she felt vulnerable and needed some extra attention. She smiled at Terrance as he walked around to the front of the car headed back to the club.

On the ride home, Kim and Stacy talked about the evening and the company they had kept.

"So? Did you enjoy yourself? Did you see how Ricky was all up on me?" Kim asked.

"Yeah, Kim. I had a blast and Ricky seems like a nice guy."

"Quit frontin' Stacy! I see you and Terrance were getting pretty cool," she said pushing Stacy in the shoulder.

"He's alright, but I ain't trying to step out on Joey. Girl, I'm about to get married."

"Well you might as well have one last dance before you vow that special shit off to one nigga for the rest of your life," Kim said jokingly.

Really Kim knew that Stacy was weak and Terrance would be the straw that broke the camel's back. When they pulled up in from of Kim's house they sat in the car for a few minutes.

"Kim, I love Joey, but a lot of times it seems like he just isn't into me."

"Do you think he is cheating?"

"I don't know or have any proof."

"Well you need to keep your options open before you get married in case he backs out, if you say he has been acting different," Kim suggested.

"Umm, alright sis. Thanks for the advice and I'll text you tomorrow cause Joey calling me now," she said blowing a kiss goodbye to her friend.

On the ride home she thought about Terrance and how smooth he was as well as good looking. There was only 15 minutes left until she would be at home so she made sure to hide his card and snap back into wifey mode.

CHAPTER TWELVE

Several days had flown by and life at home with Joey was still rocky. He had started complaining about the influence he felt that Kim had on her. He wanted to tell her about the crazy night after the party but knew that it would back fire in his face. So he continued to try to work it out without becoming to bitchy.

Days after the party at Captains, Stacy was in her office working on some pieces. She yawned as she had stayed out with Kim until 4am and then had to stay up and argue then fuck Joey to keep him happy.

She was trying to stay awake as she thought about her life and how crazy it had become. She suddenly remembered the night she was with Terrance and he'd said, "Call me when he makes you mad."

Seconds later she was dialing his number. She admired the picture on the front of his card as the phone rang. He looked so handsome and she needed to talk to someone who wouldn't judge her.

Finally he answered just as she was changing her mind, "Well thank you for calling Stacy. You've been on my mind since I last saw you. Sounds like you need a shoulder to lean on. I'm flying into Detroit on Friday, let's grab a bite to eat?" he asked.

"Uh...well," Stacy stuttered.

"Dig, shorty, it's ok. I'm a cool dude no strings attached. You can tell me what's on your mind when I text you the location. No is not an option and it'll be our little secret," he demanded.

"Ok, I'll see. Call me on Friday," she said.

"Alright then. Stay sweet shorty," he said hanging up.

Stacy laid on the couch in the studio and tried to figure out what just happened. All she knew was that she had just agreed to cheat mentally on a good man, her fiancé.

Throughout the week, Stacy was walking on egg shells wanting to back out of the date hoping he wouldn't call. On another note she couldn't stop thinking about how seductive and charming Terrance had been.

Friday morning, she got a text on her cell. :Hey pretty lady, just wanted to let you know that my plane lands at 4pm at Metro. I have a few things to set up first by 8pm. I would like to meet you at the Princess Boat. I made reservation for two on the VIP floor. See ya then – Big T:

She read the text then quickly erased it from her phone just in case Joey checked it. She knew if she got caught that it would ruin everything and change her life forever.

Later that evening she got dressed in long sundress with a pair of Louis Vuitton flats. It was a beautiful summertime ensemble. She pulled up to the large boat docked by the river front about 15 minutes early to scope out the place. She didn't need to bump into any friends or family.

Once she was sure the coast was clear she entered the huge boat and was greeted by the waiter, "Ms. Stacy your table awaits you."

"How did he know my name?" she wondered as he led her upstairs where Terrance was sitting at a large table with candles and champagne.

"Damn, you look beautiful," he said as the waiter pulled out her chair for her to sit.

After they order they engaged in conversation about the past event they shared weeks ago. While talking she noticed that she had her engagement ring on as well as her promise ring. When she glanced down at it, Terrance did as well.

"I see you love jewelry," he mentioned.

Stacy was quick on her toes as she didn't want to mention Joey to another street nigga out of fear of retaliation or an existing beef, "Yeah my mom go this for me as a reminder that I am special. She told me that if a man wants my love then he should be willing to spend more on a ring than she did."

"Understood. Are you enjoying yourself," he asked.

"Of course, now Terrance tell me about yourself," she questioned.

"It's really simple Stacy. I'm twenty years old, single with no children and I'm a resident of Miami. I come from a small family and I represent Dog Pound Squad. I'm young and rich from proper investments throughout the world. My father is am Ambassador overseas and makes sure that my family is well taken care of. Last but not least, I know what I want and how to get it," he spoke with confidence.

"I thought you were older than twenty. You are so mature for your age," she commented.

"Don't let my age run you away. I'm a fast learner and a skillful lover. You can teach me how to love in the future. For now, let's just enjoy each other's company, cool?"

They sat at the table for hours laughing and talking and Joey didn't enter her mind not once. Terrance was a treat to look at and a pleasure to be around. She figured it wasn't really cheating, she had just made a new friend.

Terrance walked her to her car and made sure to observe all her curves that the sundress was hugging as she strolled in front of him. They hugged and exchanged good nights and promised to meet again soon.

On the drive home she called Kim to check on her but she avoided any mention of her "friendly" date. At home Joey was laying on the couch playing the video game when she walked in. He immediately questioned her about her whereabouts and her cell phone. She kept her cool as he scrolled through her phone and headed back to the room to finish her back orders from work.

As the days and weeks move by, she continued living her double life without compromising her relationship at home. She continued to talk to and see Terrance and Joey was none the wiser. Not too many could achieve this level of dedication unless they were really good. Before she knew it months had gone by and her secret was still safe.

She had faltered a few times and things had come close to hitting the fan but she always kept a calm head and resolved it before it blew up. When she was out with Terrance who always wined and dined her every weekend, he always questioned her status to which she replied she was single and no one else existed in her life.

She knew she was leading him on, but she wanted to have her cake and eat it too. She had started developing feelings for him too and she knew that was out of the question. When he was in town they spent hours hanging together and growing closer. He was nice and sweet and supported all of her moves. Most of his business was in Miami so this allowed Stacy to keep a low profile from the public.

He asked a few times why she wanted to keep their relationship so low key and how come Kim couldn't know about them. She used her Christian background as excuse saying her mother would cut her off for dealing with a non-Christian. By Terrance being young and naïve to the game he agreed and remained patient and compassionate to her. They hadn't had sex so he believed she was waiting for Mr. Right.

They would hole up in a hotel and spend time together but they never even came close to having sex. He had started to notice that she had a large family and plenty of spare time but she never introduced him. He thought that was kind of strange, but accepted her desire for privacy because he loved her.

Stacy was really only his second real love and he found comfort whenever the two were together. Both of them had businesses and focused on ascertaining success.

J-Rock had been working on a new development of Town Houses that would yield him a healthy profit in Grand Rapids. This venture had taken a lot of time and energy and sometimes required nights spent out of the city. The times he was working gave her time to play. In her mind since she'd never had sex, she technically wasn't cheating.

More months passed and the seasons changed. Kim had stayed close enough to figure that Big-T and Stacy were creeping but had no hard evidence. Ricky had no reason to speak on the two so through hidden tactics and a mean head game, she finally was able to break the code of silence. With only a little bit of edge she had to wait to until the time was right to reveal the little bit of dirt she had swept up.

On Stacy and Terrance's six month anniversary, he arranged for her to fly to Miami for the weekend. It was the perfect timing because Joey was in Grand Rapids finishing up his contracts.

When she arrived she was greeted at the airport by a Bentley Coupe with a driver, who chauffeured her to one of Terrance's condos that he had especially for her. He had a full agenda that included spa days and shopping with the twenty grand he had given her upon her arrival.

Stacy loved to be pampered and all the special attention. They partied every night while the Dog Pound Crew stayed close for protection.

The weekend was going great. She called Kim a few times to check on everything in the "D." On the last night of her stay he proposed that she drop everything and stay there in Miami and live expense free for life. Though thrilled by the proposition, she respectfully declined his offer and returned home to enjoy the fruits of her labor.

The following weekend Terrance visited the "D" to meet up with some potential clients in the game that wanted to buy a share of clubs in Miami. He was well connected and respected across the globe and had access to unlimited resources. At his meeting he was introduced to a West side gangsta's wing man to view the blue prints. At this time Big-T had several deals to close to insure future business, legal and illegal.

Negotiations went smoothly and they looked forward to doing business together in the near future. "It was really cool to meet you, Fam. Be sure to tell yo mans I said let's talk. Maybe when he gets back to the city we can pop some bottles together," he joked.

"Yeah, my nigga, that sounds live as hell. Once we make this shit pop then you owe us a trip to Miami," the wing man joked back.

"Bet. Don't forget K-Doe will drop off the 50 bricks in the morning at the warehouse and the other 50 will be at the club," Big T whispered in his ear.

"Gotcha. Until then I'll call you when it's time for round two," the wing man spoke.

"Stay safe, Fam," both Big-T and Rickey said.

"Ya'll do the same," the wing man responded making his exit.

While walking to the car Rondo called J-Rock to let him know the deal was successful. Rondo had set up the deal from a connect he had met back at Stacy's art show. While overlooking the two strange outsiders at the Showcase Rondo was introduced to Ricky and Big T by a mutual friend from the east side. Neither side had knowledge of the acquaintance of Kim or Stacy to either side.

After the meeting since he was in the city, Big-T called Stacy to meet him on the 73 foot yacht he had rented off the coast of Canada. As she usual she lied to Joey and made herself available. She told him she was going to the casino for a few hours and not to wait up.

Joey had promised to help his mom and pop move into their newly built home, so he agreed knowing he would be exhausted.

Stacy sped to the dock to board the luxurious yacht that was occupied only by Big-T and the moon light. He welcomed her aboard as they lounged in the show room while he smoked a variety of exotic marijuana as they watched Belly on the projector.

Stacy never smoked weed before but since the night was so perfect she took a few puffs to relax.

"Be careful now, this shit some killa!" he warned.

Just as he said that Stacy coughed and choked trying to catch her breath.

"I told you to chill and go slow, Ma. You alright?" he asked laughing.

"Yeah boy! That shit is crazy. How do ya'll smoke that shit and function?" she asked feeling dizzy.

A few minutes later she could feel her body lifting off as the moonlight glared like a halo. The motion of the boat rocking against the waves sent her spiraling into a place where her mind had never been.

"Lay down, Ma. I got you," she heard Terrance say.

He came back with two shot of Patron to set the energy level even higher. They took several shots and laughed at DMX. Once she felt the ultimate buzz her hormones started to get the best of her. Without warning she leaned over and started kissing Terrance's neck and rubbing his chest.

He was totally surprised at how quickly the drugs and liquor had affected her. He watched as she displayed a different side of her, the side that he had desired for months.

She continued kissing him and started pulling his polo shirt off. She quickly moved to unbuckling his Fendi belt and pulling his pants off. She grabbed roughly at his boxers and located his nice hard flesh that was warm and ready to be pleased.

He relaxed and watched to see what her next move would be. Stacy grabbed his dick and placed her mouth over the shaft while rolling her tongue from side to side. This went on for a few seconds then she sucked it gently bobbing her head up and down and side to side. She gave him full view of her pleasuring skills as he watched anxiously. She jacked his dick while still sucking hard to summon his inner juices. He couldn't contain himself as he ejaculated into her mouth and she swallowed every bit of it. She continued to suck it to keep it erect. He loved the feeling he got looking down at her and to see her looking back up in her zone.

Now it was his turn to pleasure her. He quickly undressed himself and her as well. Tearing off their clothes he reached for a quick shot of Patron to help keep things flowing. He ate her pussy until she came but he wasn't finished yet. Taking control of the session Terrance flipped her over on to her stomach and pushed a pillow under her to create an arch. From behind he entered her rapidly and aggressively trying to match the rhythm of the boat rocking against the waves.

She loved every minute of it. She bit her bottom lip to keep from screaming as she clinched the sheets and took ever stroke. After twenty minutes he reached his second orgasm and released it all over her butt and tattoo's. The moment was so beautiful and exhausting that not long after, they both fell asleep, side by side until the morning.

Back at the house J-Rock had called Rondo to get Kim's number because he hadn't seen or heard from her all night. He was even more worried when Kim said, "I haven't seen her."

"What they fuck you mean? She told me that you and her were going to the casino last night!" he shouted.

"I missed her call J, so I have no idea where she is. Let me call around and try her cellphone for you," Kim said trying to be helpful.

J-Rock hung up the phone paranoid. He knew in the game he was in, she could have been kidnapped or murdered and each thought made him angrier and tense as hell.

Back on the yacht, Stacy and Terrance were awakened by the sound of the waves crashing against the boat.

"Oh shit! What time is it?" Stacy screamed jumping up and immediately looking for her clothes.

"It's a little past eight, you were sleeping so good that I didn't want to wake you," Terrance explained.

She didn't respond as she rushed around the room getting dressed as fast as she could.

"What's the rush? Why you in a panic?"

"Cause I'm fucking late! I was supposed to be home six hours ago," she said agitated.

"Late for what? Aren't you the boss?" he asked confused.

For a quick second she almost lost focus and spilled the beans. "Yeah, but I have an important meeting this morning. I'll call you later ok? I'm in a hurry," she said rushing off the boat.

Terrance watched her leave and thought there was definitely something wrong with her story.

In the car she pulled out her cell phone there were 38 missed calls from Joey and 10 from Kim. She was headed to the freeway when she decided to call Kim first to check in with her, then she would call home to Joey.

"Damn, girl! You alright?" Kim answered on the first ring.

"Yeah girl, I just fell asleep at Tee-Tee's house last night," Stacy replied.

"J-Rock is pissed the fuck off! He got my number from Rondo and called me tripping! He said you were supposed to be with me at the casino and shit. I told his ass that I never got that call cause I didn't know what else to say or what was really up," Kim said all in one breath.

"Yeah I called you but when you didn't answer I called Tee-Tee to hangout cause I was bored. Joey was in Grand Rapids last I knew," Stacy explained.

After a few minutes they hung up and she called home to face the music. She hadn't told Kim the truth and vowed never to do so. The story about Tee-Tee was a good cover up because Joey didn't know her well and neither did Kim's nosey ass.

Upon arriving at her house she was petrified about what Joey's reaction would be. She hadn't washed up yet or called to get an idea where his head was at. The ride home was quick and in no time she was walking in the house scared out of her mind.

J-Rock was sitting in the living room looking at his cell phone and observing her every move as she entered the house. Once inside, she immediately began to explain, "I'm so sorry baby! I know you are upset but I fell aslee- -."

Before she could even finish the lie, Joey slapped her to the ground. As she fell to the floor she looked up to see him in tears.

"Bitch I called Kim and every police station in the city looking for your ass," he yelled.

"I fell asleep at Tee-Tee house by mistake," she cried getting up from the floor.

"And your phone don't work, Stacy??" he yelled.

"I thought you were still in Novi helping your parents and I was too tired and buzzed to drive all the way home, Joey. If I knew you were home I would have been here. I hate coming home to a big empty house," she said trying to switch things around.

"Who the fuck is Tee-Tee?" he asked demanding an answer.

"That's Rome's wife. Kim didn't answer so I asked her to go with me downtown," she said.

J-Rock was on edge but calm enough to think about his next actions. Stacy was still trying to figure out if the story lines matched up and if he was calm enough to walk away. Deep down inside she knew that she had fucked up and over stepped her boundaries as a fiancé and a wife-to-be.

Instead of sticking around waiting on more questions and the possibility of being slapped she decided to walk to the bedroom to prepare for a long hot shower. Before she hit the stairs J-Rock grabbed her by her arm and turned her to face him. Looking into her eyes he watched her shake like a deer caught in the headlights of a truck.

Suddenly, he rubbed his hands down the front of her Nautica jogging suit stopping at her secret spot. She froze and stared as he massaged her pussy feeling to see if she was wet, open, clit hardened or smelled different. He knew his girl very well and could tell if things were different. Since she gave no resistance he removed his hand slowly without saying a word, but gave her that look that says, "I gotcha!"

Stacy immediately rushed to the shower to prepare for work and used a secret trick that women use to get their pussy completely tight. Time was of the essence and she knew she had to suck it up and pull herself together before she broke down.

She worked all day and texted Terrance to let her know that she was ok but very busy. He understood and gave her the space she needed to regain Joey's trust.

That night when he came home from working she was already in the bed waiting for him to initiate make up sex. Instead of him falling for the sex trick, J-Rock prepared for bed without speaking a word to her besides a simple, "I love you."

Stacy stayed up staring at the ceiling feeling like shit and thinking about her next move.

CHAPTER THIRTEEN

Days went by and Stacy was at work and got a call from Kim. "Hey silly, how did it go the other night?" she asked.

"It was hell, girl. We argued for a minute then he went to sleep without a word," she replied sadly.

Kim shook her head as she listened to her friends plight. She had cornered Tee-Tee at work and asked her had she talked to Stacy and she said that she hadn't talked to her in a while. Kim was searching for lost facts but would never tell Stacy she was aware that she was lying. "Well how did you do at the casino anyway?"

"Shit, I broke even then took Tee-Tee home and we had a drink or two, then it was curtains," Stacy lied. In the back of her mind she knew Kim's nosy ass was fishing for the truth for some reason. They talked for a little while longer then promised to talk later.

J-Rock was still upset and weary about the events that had taken place several nights ago. He had just started talking back to Stacy recently to avoid pushing their relationship into a spiral of mixed emotions. They had a wedding to plan soon and this wasn't helping things along. He knew in every relationship there were good times and bad but their bad had to get better and he knew that giving up was not an option.

He loved his future wife and understood that trust had to be earned. Over the next few months he would directly observe her actions with the help of Rondo. Rondo was his right hand man, whom he trusted with his money and his life. Since Rondo was in the streets 24/7 he had complete access to the gossip and a clear view of the competition.

Over the past few months Rondo had been fucking with a new connect from Miami and business was picking up. J-Rock had invested money into the right places his street time was limited to attending to all the legal aspects of the businesses.

From his success, Stacy had bought a 2 story building on Grand River and Greenfield. The large store had formerly been Kingsway. With a little secret help from Terrance she had expanded her business to a national status. Her relationship with Joey was recovering and she still had Terrance hanging on, on the side.

Living a double life was stressful yet rewarding. She was experiencing more attention, sex and money than she could handle. Both men loved her and she loved them both in return.

Keeping them separated was a challenge alone with keeping Kim at bay. Stacy had only planned to fuck with Big-T for a limited amount of time but somehow he had swept her off her feet and she had fallen in love in the process.

Whenever Terrance was in town they would spend exclusive time together in secluded places to avoid detection. She was very careful about presenting herself in public, especially with another man. At times Terrance would question her about why she picked that location or why Kim hadn't been around, seeing that she was Ricky's Detroit fling. He couldn't understand why Ricky and Kim were always hanging but never with them.

While doing business in the city with Rondo, Big-T had almost come close to meeting J-Rock in person. It's not that he needed to but it would have been nice to know the man behind the force, in the big city,

One night Big-T and Rondo were smoking a blunt together and Big-T mentioned he was about to go fuck with his city freak named Stacy. Rondo paid no attention to the name because he was fucked up. Besides he had been trailing Stacy for months and had never linked Big-T to her. Big-T was never in the city and Ricky was only around on money pick up days. He had done some real extensive research on the both of them the night of the Showcase and found nothing, which was why they were doing business together.

Stacy was outthinking everyone in the process of cheating on her lover. The crazy part is she only started to explore other options when she found out that Joey had supposedly cheated on her. Even though she never had proof, she had fallen victim to her own insecurities.

J-Rock was loyal to a fault and this made every woman in the city desire him. A nigga with money and a good heart? Who wouldn't want that? All types of women threw themselves at him but he never gave in to the temptation.

Their wedding date grew closer and their relationship seemed back on track. Their sex life was excellent even though she was tired a lot from working so much. Between all of their business ventures they were millionaires easily between their joint accounts. However in the midst of things, J-Rock wondered why Kim wasn't around anymore but he attributed that to Stacy's work schedule. He couldn't help to think back to that crazy night and wondered if Kim ever said anything to Stacy about it.

He never regretted not telling her but sometimes felt uneasy knowing that Kim had that leverage on him. Until things came to light he would continue to remain faithful and strive to be the best man he could be.

On the other hand, Stacy was in too deep to let Terrance go. They both had invested a lot of time into this strange relationship. They had been dating for a year and a half. Big-T spent countless hours and money trying to prove that he loved her more than ever. Every week he flew to Detroit to handle business with his east side squad and then to pamper his wifey.

In his mind, he was all that she knew and loved, Even though she never spent the night and always made him use protection. The only time they hadn't used protection was the first time when all inhibition and caution had been thrown to the wind.

Terrance talked to Ricky about their relationship because he was the only dude he trusted. Ricky never gave advice on how to handle Stacy bust always told him to be careful. He knew that something wasn't right with Stacy and figured she had a man. That was why she was always dipping off.

Kim was always on his head about Big-T and that had him wondering too. First he thought she wanted to get a threesome going or maybe she wanted to hook him up with another one of her friends. She never talked about Stacy but was always trying to pull info out of him about who Big-T was fucking. But then he figured if Stacy hadn't told her, then she was just fishing for info or trying to set him up. Ricky was up on the games in the city and stayed true to his boy and didn't give nobody the up's on him.

Big-T would be by himself with only a few guards following his moves from a distance. Jeopardizing his life by talking would be a risk to the both of them in the "D." So he kept Kim at bay and let Big-T and Stacy do their thing.

Big-T was young but he wasn't naïve or immune to the neglectful feeling he was having. Women threw themselves at him in Miami and he stayed loyal to Stacy and she had only visited Miami briefly. She had the best of both worlds. Two powerful men at her disposal.

That weekend Big-T was flying out to Detroit to support a party that "Wipe" was having at Club Bleu. Stacy couldn't wait to see him because it had been almost three weeks since the last visit.

He had asked Stacy to come just to see if she would talk her way out of it. Surprisingly enough she said she would come. She said she would meet him there, but that was good enough.

Stacy figured it would be cool because Joey wasn't the partying type and he didn't fuck with the east side crews so she wasn't worried. Big-T had the east side at his disposal so they would be well protected and she knew this would count as a public appearance.

She had a few days to convince Joey to let her stay out until 2am , but first she needed a fool-proof alibi. Kim wasn't a good supporter and Rome and Tee-Tee where in Louisville for the weekend. So she contacted Kayla, a close friend of hers that he knew a little about but liked as a friend for her. Once the plan was hatched and he agreed to let her go with a guaranteed curfew, it was party time...

CHAPTER FOURTEEN

The day of the party Big-T texted to be sure that Stacy was coming. :Hey sexy, just checking to see if we still on tonight. I tried to calling you but your voicemail is picking up. Hope you have a wonderful day, see ya tonight xoxoxo:

She quickly read the message then erased it but not before sending her own text: Got the message babe. Terrible reception in the building. Still coming, should be there by 10, but have to be home by 2:30 Mom is over and I have a doctors appointment in the morning. Miss you much, See ya later xoxoxoxo:

She was on her way to get her jewelry cleaned and her hair done. She made sure the messages were erased and threw her phone in her purse.

Big-T was out with his crew grabbing a quick bite to eat at Fuddruckers when he noticed a familiar face walk in with a group of women. The women were grabbing everyone's attention as they walked through the spot. When he took a closer look he saw Kim standing in the midst of the crowd, he motioned for her to come over.

"What up doe, nigga? It's been a while," she said seductively.

"Yeah, Ms. Thang, you know me all work no play," he responded trying not to notice how good she was looking.

"How is Ricky? He ain't come into town with you?

"Nahhh, he stayed back to handle some things in our town," he replied nonchalantly.

Kim noticed a few of the flyers that his crew had been handing out. 'What's this about?"

He waved to his boy to give her a few flyers. "This is a party that I'm sponsoring with 'Wipe" at Club Bleu. You need to come and bring all those fine women you have with you to represent. Hit Stacy up and fall through tonight," he suggested while adjusting his Cartier frames.

"You like Stacy, huh?" she said with a smile.

"You already know," he laughed.

"Alright I'll see what's these hoes have up tonight and we might fall through," she said slyly. Her suspicions were raging now that he had requested Stacy to come. Could she be right about these two?

Later that night Kim called Stacy to invite her to the party but every call went to voicemail. She just assumed J-Rock had her on lock down or something.

An hour before the party started Big-T was riding in his Benz CL600 when he decided to hit up Rondo.

"What up doe fool? You in the city?" Rondo answered.

"Yeah, fool. What you got up for the night?"

"Shit, about to find me a hoe to bang or somethin'. What's good?" he answered.

Big-T filled him in on the party. He assured Rondo that even though he knew he wasn't with the east side that he didn't have anything to worry about. He would be safe with him.

"Yeah man, that's straight. Bleu isn't east side , it's down town but I'm cool everywhere, Fam. I'll fall through but you gotta get my girl in too," he stated.

"Cool you know she get the same VIP treatment too," Big-T said.

"Nahh, not my hoe nigga, I'm talking about that toolie," he enlightened Big-T.

"Oh shit, nigga! This "d" slang out the gate. Don't panic, I'll meet you at the door so she'll be good," Big –T laughed.

At the club he waited for everyone to arrive. Of course everyone was fashionably late. Stacy pulled up a little late wearing a Chanel jogging suit with matching jewelry. She quickly made her way to VIP to enter the jam packed section. He locked eyes with her as they greeted with a hug and brief kiss. All eyes were on them and he felt like the proud owner of a Bentley.

The club was extremely live as people danced and mingled, while DJ Drunken Master rocked the latest tunes. Big-T had a table up on the top floor so that he could watch the entry way to the club and rear exit. He heard his name paged over the loud speaker.

"I'll be back baby. Chill and drink up," he said to Stacy.

At the front door a group of 6 girls all dressed nice and looking like models.

"Damn, bout time nigga!" Kim joked and shouted over the music.

Big-T smiled and whispered to the security guard, "They wit me."

The women all said thanks and entered ready to set it off.

Big-T then returned back to Stacy after letting Kim and her girls in and showing them to the bar. "Hey Boo, yo girl Kim just showed up deep as hell," he shouted over the music.

"Kim? She's here?" she asked nervously.

"Yeah, didn't she tell you I saw her earlier and asked her to come?" he asked.

Stacy almost fell out of the tall chair, she had to think fast to avoid a situation.

"I told her to call you so that ya'll could come together," he said.

"She did call, but I forgot to call her back."

"Did you tell her I was coming or that I was already here?" she asked calmly.

"Nah, I figured ya'll knew about the party and who was coming. She downstairs at the bar, you want her?"

Stacy was thrown off for a minute and thought that if she stayed up in VIP that she would be safe. "Maybe Kim was here because she thought that Ricky would show up?" Stacy thought to herself. She knew that show had to go on and she needed to keep a calm head.

Around 30 minutes later the club was even more packed just as the 12am Showcase featuring "The Chedda Boyz" was about to start. Everyone crowded around the stage for the performances as Stacy hid upstairs to try to avoid any contact. Right after the performance Big-T was summoned to the door again. He left Stacy for a minute wondering why she hadn't tried to find or talk to Kim. "It must be a girl thing," he thought to himself.

He saw Rondo standing at the door and motioned for them to let him through. Rondo waved him all the way over and whispered, "My dog is strapped."

Big-T waved them off and just like that Rondo and his man Doc were walking into the club.

"Yeah I got some bottles and models up top in the VIP. Here are two passes," he said giving them access to VIP.

"Alright we gon browse the land real quick then I'll be up there to kick it with you," Rondo said scanning the room.

Big-T had strolled back to the VIP to check on Stacy as the DJ blasted "Gator City" by Rockbottom.

While storming to the bar, Doc wearing a head full of dreads tapped Rondo and alerted him to a group of females dancing in a circle. Rondo glanced over at them but before he moved several drinks had to invade his system. After downing a few shots of Remy XO, Rondo approached the crowd of females only to notice Kim in the middle shaking her money maker.

She turned around and saw Rondo backing that thing up. She smiled and danced over to him, 'What's up Boo?"

"What's up lil Kim, see you networking that good shit," he joked.

"Boy shut up! Who you here with?"

"My dude over there getting his game over there with that redbone and my nigga Big-T got me hooked up with VIP," he said pulling her into him.

"Big-T? That's my boy!" she said.

"Yeah, we go back a bit. I'm about to head up to kick it with him now," he said pointing up top.

"Fuck it, I'll roll witcha. Shit free up there," she smiled.

They took the long way around to reach the section to avoid crossing the dance floor. Security allowed them past and they found Big-T at a large table in the back. He was watching the basketball game on the flat screen with a gang of dudes around him. When they got close enough they saw a female sitting on his lap. His bodyguard tapped him on the shoulder to let him know that someone wanted to talk to him.

"What up nigga?" Big-T said to Rondo leaning over to shake his hand. He noticed Kim standing behind him looking strange.

"Damn T, I didn't know you knew crazy ass Rondo," Kim said.

"Yeah, this my dude. I see ya'll know each other huh? Big-T said surprised.

Five feet away Stacy heard Terrance talking to someone but paid it no mind since he had been getting up to talk to people all night. That was until she heard Terrance say, "Hey Boo, come here! I want you to meet somebody."

She slowly rose and turned around and couldn't believe who she saw. Her jaw dropped, just as both and Rondo realized who she was.

"Hey Stacy! What you doing here girl?" Kim asked shocked as ever.

Rondo almost pulled out his gun and started shooting everyone around, but he kept his head and played it cool. It was too much heat up there to do anything silly. Big-T was a made nigga and if he acted an ass, death would have called him home real quick.

"Hey Kim! It's nice to see you could make it. What up doe, Rondo?" Stacy greeted them both with a pale face.

"Damn, Boo. You know my nigga Rondo too?" Big-T asked.

"Yeah, I've seen him with Kim a few times," she replied avoiding making eye contact with anyone.

"Yeah, it's a small world, ain't it Stacy?" Rondo said grabbing his waist.

"Then let's pop a few bottles since we all Fam," Big-T said signaling the waitress.

It was the most awkward moment in all of their lives, other than Terrance who was oblivious to the real situation. Stacy stood there looking crazy while Rondo was steaming from the ears. Kim was still shocked and waiting for the breaking point. Not only was she cheating, but with a nigga that ran the same streets as her man.

"Alright fam, I gotta shoot a move," Rondo said after they had a few drinks. I'll hit you up later though, fa'sho!" He didn't want to start a war over some pussy or mess up the connect but he had to get away from the situation to get his head straight.

"Cool, my nigga. Make sure you hit me," Big-T said.

"Catch you later, Stacy," Rondo said with a smirk.

"Yeah, girl. Be safe and call me when you get home," Kim laughed openly.

Stacy ignored them both and was trying to formulate a plan in her head. She had to get home before Rondo called Joey. She told Terrance she had to leave too because her period was coming down. Time was on her side because as soon as she said that a fight broke out on the dance floor. Some cats from Chalmers had gotten into a beef with some niggas off of East Warren and all hell broke out.

Big-T had his bodyguard walk her to her car while he attended to the scuffle that was ruining his event. In the car Stacy drove slow and tried to call Kim and Rondo to explain her version of the strange night. Neither of them picked up the phone, so she called Joey to check the vibe. He didn't answer so she really started to panic.

When she arrived to the house she saw his car was there but all the lights were out in the house. She quietly entered the house and re-set the alarm. She saw Joey laid out on the couch with the controller still in his hand, and the video game on the screen of the television. She heard the alert on his phone and picked it up. 17 missed calls and 15 were from Rondo.

"Damn, damn, damn!" she mumbled under her breath.

She knew it would be a rough night if he woke up so she quietly turned his cell phone off to avoid any more calls from Rondo and she would sleep extra light and get up early to fix shit. She got in the bed and prayed that God would shine some type of favor on her by the morning.

CHAPTER FIFTEEN

In the morning, she woke up before Joey and started cooking breakfast. The smell of buttermilk pancakes and turkey bacon filled the house as Joey roused from the coma he was in.

He quickly took a shower and got dressed to head downstairs to eat. He had a busy day planned and good breakfast would be a great start to the day.

"Good morning, sexy," he greeted her with a kiss.

"I made your favorite, honey. How did you sleep?" she asked calmly.

"Damn my battery must have died last night," he said turning his phone on. "What the fuck? Rondo called me 20 times!" He tried listening to the messages but couldn't really hear him so he dialed his number.

Stacy stiffened up as she listened to them talking. She prayed Rondo wouldn't tell.

"Listen J-Rock, we gotta talk, man," Rondo started, then he turned to the side and asked Kim to give him a minute. She got up and went downstairs for a drink of water. "Listen my nigga. You my family and no matter what goes on in your personal life, know that I'm with you 100 percent."

"Nigga! What up? Talk to me!" Joey yelled.

"Man, last night I was in Club Bleu with Kim and Doc, my man Big-T that I told you that is getting us the order on the low was there. He was hosting a party for "Wipe" and while I was there I bumped into your girl Stacy."

"And," J-Rock interrupted,

"Man she was all up on old boy and he introduced her as his Boo," Rondo explained.

Stacy was listening and though she couldn't hear Rondo's side she knew shit had just hit the fan.

"Man, she fucking old boy and she played me and Kim like we were some lames. I wanted to do my thang but I decided to let you call the shots on this one. Damn, man, I'm sorry," Rondo ended.

Joey was sitting at the table in the kitchen and reached for his .45 Caliber handgun at his waist and told his boy he would hit him back later.

"Bitch you playing me like that?" he screamed at Stacy as he jumped up and put the gun to her head.

She was caught off guard but could feel the cold metal pressed up against her skull. "I can explain Joey! Please don't hurt me," she pleaded with him.

"Explain what, Bitch? You about to marry me and your cheating ass playing me?" he yelled again.

"It was a mistake Joey! I need you, but you wasn't thinking about me, it was always about your money," she said crying.

"I should blow your fucking head off," he said crying and confused.

She grabbed his hand and fell to her knees. In his other hand the gun stayed aimed at her nose.

"I'm so sorry baby I was lost and lonely," she cried. "Please don't do it. Please, I'm so sorry."

Joey stood there in disbelief thinking that the woman he gave his life to and stayed loyal to had betrayed him. His mind was cloudy and tears filled his eyes. "Why me? After all I've given you Stacy?

He lowered the gun and stormed out of the house without saying another word. Stacy laid on the floor crying. She knew that her life had just taken a turn for the worst. Trust, loyalty and several years of dedication had been thrown out of the window because of one bad decision.

Once she gathered herself she called Kim and asked her to come over. She didn't want to be alone but she didn't want to leave because she was sure he wouldn't allow her back in. She had made her bed and was going to have to lie in, dead or alive.

Kim had been with Rondo all night and said she would stop by for a minute because she really didn't want to be anywhere near the house when Joey came back.

Joey was running the full gamut of emotions as he drove downtown to check into a room. He was confused and not sure if he could be to blame for this craziness, but then he was so angry from the betrayal that he couldn't think straight. He just wanted to be left alone. He checked in using a fake ID so no one would know that he was there. He needed time to sort out his feelings and think everything through.

He wasn't sure whether he should leave or stay with Stacy. He had so much invested in the relationship that he couldn't believe that she would risk it all for some attention.

Back at the house, Kim and Stacy sat in the living room talking about all that had transpired over the last few months. Kim decided since the cat was out of the bag, then her job was done. It would only be a matter of time before Joey needed a shoulder to lean on and she would be right there for him.

Stacy paced the floor trying to figure out how you fix disloyalty or betrayal. What could she do to fix this? She had tried calling Joey for hours but her calls went straight to voicemail, so she knew that it was turned off. She just wanted to hear his voice and know that he was alright.

Later, Kim had gone home and Stacy laid in the bed staring at the ceiling. It was past midnight and she was really beginning to worry about Joey.

While at the room, he too was wide awake staring at the ceiling. Not only had she cheated but she had cheated with his connect. He wanted revenge on both of them but he knew it wasn't worth the repercussions.

He stayed at the room for several days, avoiding all calls until he was ready to face the fact that things had changed. Stacy cried every day and checked every hotel, hospital and police station. She even called Kim and Rondo to help to aid in the search for J-Rock. They weren't any help.

Days turned into nights and it had been four long days without a word from him. Stacy had been on pins and needles trying to figure out his whereabouts. She had talked to Terrance a few times briefly, but avoided any physical contact. She was not leaving the house or her phone unattended.

She simply told Terrance that things at home were stressful and she needed a few days to sort shit out. On the fifth day of his absence, Joey decided that he had calmed down and wanted to make his next move.

While eating a breakfast delivered by room service, Joey picked up his cell to call Rondo. Rondo was at the office keeping shit in order until he resurfaced. He knew as a friend that this was hard on J-Rock and allowed him to reach out on his own.

"What up doe my people? You straight?" Rondo asked.

Yeah fam, just had to lay low for a minute to get my mind right," J-Rock responded.

"I feel ya. Yo girl been going crazy."

"I can dig it. She'll be alright. Dig, won't you grab a zone out of the desk and head down to the Marriott on Jefferson, so we can kick it," J-Rock responded.

"Fo sho my nigga, give me about 30 minutes and I'll lock up and shoot down," Rondo reassured him.

While Rondo was in route, Joey called Stacy who was at the house alone thinking the worst.

"Hello? Babe? You ok?" she answered anxiously.

"Yeah, I'm cool. Don't panic but at some point we need to talk," he said with no emotion in his voice.

"I know Bae, I fucked up. Please come home so we can talk. Please forgive me," she begged.

"I'll get at cha'," he said and hung up the phone.

She was happy to know that he was ok and that he was even considering talking to her. That was a start but she knew she had a long, long way to go.

Joey waited in the room until Rondo called and he gave him the room number so he could come up. Rondo came in and gave him some dap, "What it do, Fam?"

"Man, trying to figure this shit out, dude," he said sitting down.

Rondo pulled out the ounce of exotic weed and started rolling blunts. Smoke filled the air and their lungs as they talked about the past week's events.

"Man I understand your situation, Bro, and if you say the word I'll dead the dude for the violation," Rondo spoke angrily.

"Nahh, Fam. He ain't know about me as a person. If he did then it's still all on her for being weak," J-Rock said.

'Dog, I know you love lil' sis and all. I'm ya man from way back. All I can say is that no matter what you decide, I gotcha back. I can show you a lot of shit in life but I can't show how or who to love," Rondo said.

Joey just looked at the ground, shaking his head. He took a strong pull from the blunt and looked at his right hand man, "You're right lil Bro. Shit is crazy and I hate losing at anything, especially life. I guess this situation will only make us stronger as a unit. Truthfully, I feel so betrayed and it's hard to forgive disloyalty. Maybe I'll go home and talk to her crazy ass," J-Rock suggested.

"Do that Fam and once you are ready to get back to work, let me know. I won't say shit to ole boy, that way business is still on point, ya dig?" Rondo stated smiling.

"Cool. I'll keep you posted. I'll politic with you later bout that too."

They dapped and Rondo left giving J-Rock time to prepare for the showdown at home.

CHAPTER SIXTEEN

When he pulled up to the house thing seemed really quiet. It was hard not to replay the events that had occurred the night that he had ran away from a murder case. Once he pulled in the garage, he noticed Stacy's car hadn't moved. He took a deep breath before entering the house.

Inside, Stacy laid on the king sized bed watching, "Waiting to Exhale." She glanced up and saw Joey standing in the doorway just staring at her with a blank expression.

"You scared me," she whispered, still unsure of where his mind was at.

"I know it's late, but we really need to talk," he said.

Stacy jumped off the bed and went to hug him but he stopped her in her tracks. She was initially shocked at his reaction then hurt. She looked at him as he sat down on the edge of the bed looking her in the eye.

"Ok, explain to me how this all happened," he requested calmly.

Stacy took a deep breath and told him the whole story. How they had met, how long they had been talking and everything. She knew she was hurting Joey, but he had to know.

She continued to detail the trips, money and sex which led her eyes to fill with tears as she watched her story tearing her lover to pieces. She knew that confessing it all would give her a clean heart but a dirty record for certain.

Joey interrupted her a few times with a question or two on something that he wasn't clear on. After he had listened to the entire story, he realized that he had played a small part in neglecting his wife to be. By paying so much attention to the front door, he had allowed someone to enter his castle through the back door. Forgiving her would take a lot of time and action, but he knew he couldn't live without her.

"Why couldn't you just come to me, like a woman Stacy?"

"It all happened so fast and the extra attention made me feel wanted," she responded.

"How can I sleep at night knowing I can't trust you? It sounds like you are in love with this cat, who is also a business partner of mine," he questioned her.

"I'm not in love with anyone but you. I had feelings for him but that is all. I'll show you that I want to marry you and that you're all I need to be complete," she cried.

Joey listened and tried to believe her but he knew that a two year affair just couldn't end like that, but he wanted his relationship to work. After talking for several hours they both were tired and decided to finish the discussion in the morning. They slept apart, but peacefully all night.

The next morning Joey had made his mind up. "Stacy, getting back to how we were before is going to take some time," he acknowledged.

"I know, just please don't treat me different. I made a mistake and I'm willing to work to regain your trust and heart back."

"I'm glad you said that! First you need to get wit cha man and kill that bullshit. Second, change your number and I'll change all the codes to the house, and lastly I'm letting you know this is our last shot at being a family. I can't worry about getting my head blown off cause you want to play both sides of the fucking fence. This dude knows Rondo and can easily find out who I am. It's not a game, Stacy. Get this shit in order and quick!" he demanded.

Stacy was scared to death as she replied, "I'll get it right, Joey."

Joey left to catch up on his business. Stacy was left to try to figure out how to make this right. She was literally torn between two lovers but she loved Joey more. She didn't want to hurt Terrance but it was the only way that she could get her old life back that she now so desperately wanted.

The next few days passed by with her treading lightly around the house and waiting for the right moment to call Terrance. She and Joey hadn't had sex yet and she knew exactly why that was. But she totally understood. It was time to make that call, to make it right.

CHAPTER SEVENTEEN

Big-T was beginning to wonder how Stacy was doing. He hadn't verbally talked to her in a couple of weeks and had only text her to give her some space to get her family situation in order. But he was missing his little lady and decided to fly into town for a surprise visit.

Once his plane landed, he jumped into the CL600 that was waiting for him. Dressed in Dolce & Gabanna with a pair of Ferragamo loafers, he headed straight to Stacy's office off of Greenfield.

Inside the large building Stacy sat at her desk taking notes from a conference call that she was on.

"Excuse Ms. Moore, there is a gentleman here to see you," the cute receptionist said sticking her head in the room.

"Give me one second and I'll be right out," she said. After her call ended she headed to the lobby and was shocked to see Terrance looking very debonair and handsome.

She knew they had to talk but this wasn't the time or the place. "Hey, what are you doing her," she asked.

"Look at you all professionally dressed, looking like a sexy ass business woman," he responded.

"Thanks but I didn't know you were coming," she said.

"I was missing you and I wanted to check on you in person to be sure you were ok," he said.

The receptionist buzzed the buzzer when someone knocked and was greeted by several men wearing Danny's Floral t-shirts came walking in. They each carried a dozen roses with balloons and the last one was holding a life-sized teddy bear and a card.

"Just in time," Terrance said. "These are for you."

Stacy stood there lost for words and at that moment all the feeling she held deep inside for him came to light, "Thanks babe."

"Anything for you, I just had to see you and …"

Stacy interrupted as she finally snapped back to her senses. The game was over and she had to tell Terrance the truth. "Terrance, we need to talk."

"About what?"

"Listen, I'll call you tonight so we can clear some things up," she said.

"What's the matter, Stacy?"

"I gotta get back to work. I'll call you when I close up," she said looking at the floor.

"Just come down to the Hyatt downtown after work," he suggested.

"Ok, I'll see you later."

She hugged him and gave him a kiss on the cheek. He left confused and a little worried. He wondered was she pregnant or did she have some type of shit? He had no idea what was up with her but he hurried to the room to await her arrival.

At the office Stacy was nervous about meeting Terrance and hoped that he would understand without holding a grudge. A couple of hours later after she closed the office she called Joey to let him know she would be home late.

She popped in the new Beyoncé cd and tried to relax before the emotional roller coaster ride. Inside the hotel Big-T talked on the phone with Ricky, who had stayed behind in Miami to handle business there.

Stacy clicked in asking for the room number, "I'll send Tone down to walk you up," he told her.

Minutes later she was walking into the suite. He dismissed Tone and told him to hold down the front. Tone briskly exited the room to secure the floor.

Stacy sat down and Terrance made them both a drink at the minibar. He looked so handsome and her heart melted as she watched him. The chemistry they shared was undeniable but after tonight, things would be totally different.

"Ok sexy, since you're here and I'm guessing it's not to spend the night, why don't you tell me what's on your mind?" he said handing her a drink and sitting down next to her.

"Well Terrance, I know you are not going to want to hear this. I haven't been completely honest with you, from day one. I hope you'll understand what I'm about to say, but please know that my love for you is strong."

"What's up Stacy, talk to me?" he said.

"I've been engaged to my fiancé for four years," she said quietly.

"What the fuck is you saying?" he shouted.

"Please listen."

Terrance stood up and paced the room.

"I never meant for this to go this far. One we started hanging out I fell in love with you. I know it was wrong but I couldn't help my feelings," she said.

"Damn! I can't believe this shit!" he yelled.

Tone came into the room to check on his boss, "Everything alright in here?"

"We cool! Close the fucking door!" Terrance yelled.

"Terrance, my fiancé sound out about us through a mutual friend and things got out of hand."

"So really the only reason you telling me this shit is cause you got caught up?"

"It's not like that Terrance! I was torn between the two of you. I love you, but my heart belongs to him," she cried.

'Ok so what's the deal now? All the shit I been through with you is over? I gave you my all Stacy, my fucking all. So who is this fucking nigga and why me?" he asked balling his fist up.

"Calm down Terrance! His name doesn't matter. All I can say is sorry for putting you through this shit. I'm hurting too Terrance, but we can't do this anymore."

"So just fuck me huh? Just fuck me? All the time and money I put into this fake ass relationship means nothing, huh?" he questioned with tears in his eyes.

Stacy saw that he was hurt and his temper was flaring so she felt bad breaking the news to him this way.

She stood up to show comfort by wiping his rears and hugging him gently to ease the pain.

Suddenly he pushed her away and started throwing things around the room. He started punching the walls and at the air. Stacy was scared as hell and wanted to leave without making matters worse.

Terrance was outraged about the entire incident. He felt like he had been played like a fool from the start. He tried to calm down as thoughts of beating the shit out of her swirled around in his mind.

She could feel the tension so she reacted quickly to calm him down. No one knew where she was or who she was with and she knew Terrance had the power to kill her and get away with it.

She walked up and embraced him and this time he didn't push her away. She melted in his arms as he held her strongly and they engaged in a sensual kiss. If it was one thing that she knew would calm a nigga down, it was the pussy.

She continued to defuse the situation by seducing him. She led him over to the bed and laid him down.

Having sex wouldn't be the smartest thing she could do but it was damn sure pleasurable.

She removed her bar clothes quickly which surprised Terrance and he let his guard down. The silhouette of her naked body on top of his had him going crazy. He gave up control as she pulled down his boxer shorts and grabbed his hard on. She raised up and sat down allowing him to enter her soft, wet, tight pussy and rocked until she was tired. Then she switched to the reverse cowgirl position to allow the view for him to widen.

This brought the tension down but did not change that both of their lives had changed. Laying in the bed, they both looked at each other knowing their "thing" had ended.

"I love you, Stacy," Terrance said sadly.

"I love you too. I hope you can forgive me one day. I'm sorry, but I needed to have you inside of me one last time," she replied.

"It's cool. This is going to be hard for me. I'm lost without you, but I'll try to move on."

Stacy knew her job was done and was happy that she could leave on good terms. Big-T on the other hand wasn't too optimistic about letting go that easy.

Stacy got up and went to the bathroom to wash up then he walked her out to the hallway to call Tone to come back up. He quietly told him to follow Stacy home to get the location. He then told him to call Keith to take his post for the rest of the night. He had to find out who was this nigga that he had lost out to.

As Stacy drove home, she called Kim to talk. She was completely unaware that she was being followed. When she pulled up to the house, Joey was sitting on the porch smoking a blunt.

She ended her call with Kim and got out of the car, "Hey Boo," she said.

"Where you been?" he asked directly.

"At work, then I shot to drop Kim off some flyers that we printed up," she responded.

"Alright, I'll be in shortly," he said slightly dismissive.

"Dang, I love you," she said jokingly.

"I love you too," he said covering the mouthpiece of his cell.

On the opposite side of the street Tone sat quietly observing the whole scene. He phoned Big-T with the news.

"I'm at that special joint and seen ya man's chilling too," he reported.

"Cool, don't so shit. Keep the info and I'll catch up with you later at the club," Big-T demanded.

"Ok Boss, catch ya later," Tone spoke while hanging up. He pulled off slowly from the curb and drove past the house.

J-Rock couldn't see inside the truck but did realize that he had never seen this truck around the area before tonight. Since he was on the phone with Rondo he gave all the intel to him, for back up reasons.

That night J-Rock and Stacy engaged in a long sexual joy ride as she gave him the special treatment. Making love to her man always gave her a sense of relief. After hours of making love they fell asleep in each other's arms until the morning.

CHAPTER EIGHTEEN

Several weeks had past and Stacy and Joey's relationship was heading in the right direction. She was relieved from the extra stress of living two different lives and he was enjoying having her undivided attention. Letting the past go was still kinda hard for the both, but growing into the future was their main focus.

Kim and Rondo were around to lend an ear or be supportive of their true love and to help with the planning of the wedding. Rondo was aware of the bond that Stacy and Big-T had shared and therefore kept his ear to the street to see if she was creeping back. They were still in business with Big-T so he had to be extra alert and observant. On the other hand Kim still wanted Joey for herself but figured it was best to stay in her lane until the next opportunity presented itself. She had love for her girl and actually felt bad about seeing her life almost destroyed over lust and bad decisions.

But her desire for Joey never let her miss an opportunity to flirt with him to let him know that she was there for him too. J-Rock had been loyal and remained dedicated to his fiancée but often wondered about how she handled ending it with the other dude.

Stacy had never mentioned how she broke the news to Terrance. Joey had an idea when it had taken place but he couldn't be sure. He was just happy that it was over.

After a few months Stacy began to wonder why she had never heard back from Terrance. Had he gotten over her that easy? Had he been playing her from the start? Whenever she saw a flyer for a party he was hosting, or heard Kim talking about Ricky she would think of him even though she knew she had done the right thing.

One day while she was at work her cell phone rang with a blocked number, "Hello this is Stacy. How may I help you?"

"I love you," the male voice said.

"Excuse me? Who is this?" she asked, then the caller hung up.

"Was that Terrance?" she thought to herself.

She continued working without giving the call any real thought. Later that night while she prepared to lock up her phone rang again with a blocked number.

"Hello?"

"Hey can you talk?" the voice on the other line asked.

"Terrance? Is this you?" she asked cautiously.

"I miss you so much. This shit is killing me not to talk to you."

"But, you know I can't do this anymore, Terrance."

"I'll let you keep your fiancé, Stacy. I just need to have a little time with you," he pleaded.

"I can't Terrance. I'm sorry but we gotta let it go."

"It's so hard, baby. My life isn't the same without you. Can I come see you?" he asked.

"No, no, no. That's not a good idea. I have to go, Terrance. I'm sorry. Please don't call anymore," she said and hung up the phone.

As she walked to her car she noticed a black SUV pulling out of parking lot in back. She only noticed it because of the pitch black tinted windows and dealer plate on the back.

On the way home her mind wandered as usual to the affair that she and Terrance had had. It had been two and a half months since they'd seen each other and the phone calls today had really creeped her out. She was proud of herself for cutting it short. This was no time to fuck up again with the wedding only eight months away.

Once she made it home she called Kim to tell her what had happened.

"Damn, Stacy! That's some crazy shit! You know he been in town the past couple of days with Ricky," Kim stated.

"Nah, I haven't been in touch with him but he sounded really weird today," she said.

"Well just stay away from him and focus on your planning. I'll call you tomorrow when I'm on my way to the shop," Kim told her before hanging up.

She prepared dinner for Joey and Rondo who was over watching the game. While she was bringing them their plates her phone rang again with the blocked number. She knew it was him again and if she answered it all hell would break loose. But if she didn't answer then Joey would think she was hiding something.

She picked it up and prayed for good results, "Hello?"

"Stacy I need to see you," Terrance said.

"Hey girl, what you still doing up," she said.

"Meet me at my room," he asked.

"Naw girl, I'm at home about to call it a night," she said calmly into the phone as she walked back into the kitchen. When she got back in the kitchen she was furious. 'Terrance you have to stop calling me. I'm at home with my family," she begged.

"I don't give a fuck! What about me?" Big-T shouted into the phone.

"I can't help you. Stop calling me please or I will get my number changed," she whispered then hung up.

She knew that changing her numbers wasn't really an option with her whole client base having that number. She just prayed that he would stop calling before Joey noticed anything. She thought about telling Joey what was happening but didn't want to open the old wound.

On the other side of town Terrance was furious. His entire squad and family couldn't believe that he had allowed himself to be played. He had to get her back into his life somehow and he was willing to do or pay whatever for it. After calling her phone back several times to no avail, he decided he would surprise her at work in a few days.

Big-T and Rondo had just finished doing a major deal at a local club on the west side. Rondo had observed Big-T in his CL600 but also noticed a large black truck following him as they pulled off. This struck him kind of odd because he remembered J-Rock telling him that he had seen one patrolling in his neighborhood. He tried to peer through the tinted windows but had no luck seeing the driver, so he took a mental note of the vehicle.

Big-T wanted to win Stacy's heart again by sweeping her off her feet. While she was at work in her office, her receptionist came to the door, "Boss lady, you have a bunch of flowers and candy waiting on you downstairs," she said excitedly.

"What?" Stacy asked looking up from her laptop. She got up and walked down to the main floor to see what all the excitement was about. The lobby was filled with wonderful gifts. There were two toy poodles parading around with bow ties on.

"The delivery guy dropped them off with no card or anything," the receptionist said rubbing one of the puppies.

"Joey is so sweet," she said aloud. She had been asking for a small pet for company. This really made her feel special. Since there was no card attached she assumed they were from him.

She tried to call him to thank him but her call went to voicemail, so she called Kim to brag about the magnificent gifts that he had given her.

At closing she packed up all the gifts and hurried home. As she pulled into the garage, Joey was coming out to make a run. The little dogs jumped out to greet him.

"Aww, where you get the cute little dogs," he asked.

Her mind went blank as she started to say, "From you," but thought wiser. "These are Kim's. I'm doggy sitting."

"Don't let them fuck up the crib. This is a test for you," he said giving her a kiss and getting into his car.

Joey pulled off and Stacy fell to her knees. Now she knew the gifts weren't from him. Why wouldn't he leave her the fuck alone!? She called Kim immediately to put her up on game in case Joey or Rondo called her to confirm the story. Terrance was really tripping and she was scared as hell.

The next day she called him and told him not to send anymore gifts and that she was donating the dogs to a local shelter. He was upset as expected but not more than she was. She hung up out of breath after telling him off.

Kim met her at the office for lunch. They talked about all the crazy things that had transpired over the past few months. During their conversation, Stacy felt a little sick and had to retreat to the bathroom to vomit.

"You ok?" Kim asked concerned.

"Yeah, that sweet and sour chicken didn't sit well on my stomach," she replied.

"Well I hope you feel better, honey. I gotta get back to the shop to help close up. Rome be tripping if I don't pull my weight," Kim said.

"Ok, trust me, I know how that nigga is. Plus I'm gon gone ahead and close up too, I don't feel good."

While letting Kim out, Stacy noticed that black SUV driving down Grand River again. Since her stomach was hurting she decided to close up quickly to get some rest. While locking up, call came through from Terrance, unblocked.

"Hello?"

"Damn, baby. I know you getting tired of me calling but I just have to talk to you," he demanded.

She headed to her car, "Ok Terrance let's talk, but after this discussion you have to stop calling!"

On her ride home, she tried to answer all his questions and concerns to help ease his pain. She really didn't have the answer that he wanted to hear but she tried to appease him as much as she safely could.

She was so tuned into the conversation that she didn't notice him following closely behind her. He tried to keep her on the phone but when she pulled into the garage, she ended the conversation abruptly.

Inside the house Joey was chilling watching Scarface on the big screen. She loved this movie and since she was feeling under the weather, she went to change to come back and watch it with him.

"Hey baby, what you been doing all day," she asked.

"Shit, missing you. Why you home so early?" he asked.

"My stomach was messed up after eating lunch with Kim so I closed up to relax and get some medicine."

"Come over here so I can take care of you, sexy," he said pulling her down on the couch with him.

As soon as she sat down her phone rang with a blocked number. She couldn't believe her luck! She jumped back up to answer it and headed to the bathroom for the medicine cabinet. Joey had the surround sound on so he knew she couldn't hear it, so he thought nothing of her getting up to leave.

She answered the phone angrily, "What?!"

"Stacy can we meet for 30 minutes, please? I'm fucked up baby," Terrance cried into the phone.

"Listen, you can't call me anymore. I'm at home with my dude!" she whispered.

"I know."

"You know? What do you mean?" she asked.

"You got a choice, either you come out with me now or I'm coming in to get you," he demanded sniffling into the phone.

"Terrance, now is not a good time. I'm on my period, boy," she said looking out the bathroom window.

"Ok since you acting like that and you're the reason why I'm feeling this way...we'll do it your way. I love you," he said hanging up.

Seconds later she heard a loud bang coming from down stairs while she was looking for the Pepto.

Joey was on the couch half sleep when the loud sound echoed over the movie playing. Once his eyes focused all he saw was a huge man rushing towards him with a gun pointed at him.

The gunman screamed, "I hate you nigga!" and aimed for his head while pulling the trigger.

Blood ran down Joey's face as he lie dead on the couch from the single gunshot. The intruder then raced around the house looking for Stacy. She had heard the gunshot and quickly ran to check on Joey. When she got to the top of the stairs she saw a familiar face looking back at her.

'Terrance! What are you doing? Oh my God!" she screamed.

Terrance had the look of a mad man in his eyes as he aimed the gun at Stacy. She ran to hide in the bedroom where the gun was stashed in the drawer. But she was seconds too late. Terrance was right behind her.

"Please, I love you. Why are you doing this shit?" she screamed.

He looked back her with a blank face and tears in his eyes and pulled the trigger several times.

Stacy fell to the floor holding her neck and gasping for air. Terrance stood over her and whispered, "I love you," as he released one more shot into her abdomen.

Stacy slowly lost consciousness as the vision on Terrance holding the gun started fading away.

Slowly he turned away and started back down the stairs. When he reached the bottom of the stairs, the door crashed open and a police officer ran in.

"Drop your weapon, now! Drop it or we'll be forced to help you," the office yelled.

Terrance knew his life was over for good. He had made peace with his decision and couldn't live without Stacy anyway. "I'm going to jail and the love of my life is gone. Fuck it! I'll see her in the afterlife," was his last thought as he put the gun in his mouth and pulled the trigger.

CHAPTER NINETEEN

It had been 37 days since Stacy had been admitted to the hospital. She was in a coma and everyone was worried about her condition. Her mother slept by her side every night. Kim came to visit every day with Rondo who vowed to support his best friend's wishes.

The tragic event had caught them both off guard and neither one knew that Big-T was the shooter. He had a fake id and the police weren't releasing any information to them about the perp anyway.

Joey's family would come and visit and offer Ms. Moore any support they could. It was hard for them as well, having buried their son a few weeks prior.

In the hood, the entire Fenkell Boy's crew sought revenge for the death of their homeboy, but little information was known at the time.

Detectives Freeman and Ross had continued to work hard following numerous leads and updates on the case. Checking in on Stacy was a regular routine that allowed them to stay close in case any progress happened.

As a true friend, Kim continued to run Stacy's business and Rondo continued Joey's. Life was hard for them all but Ms. Moore had it worst.

She was awakened one day by the sounds fast beeps from the monitor. While she adjusted her vision to the surroundings, she saw her daughter's eyes fluttering. She sat up to watch closer. Figuring that this was just another side effect from the comas she watched closer. Seconds after Stacy moved her hand to feel her stomach as the beeping sounds became louder. That's when Ms. Moore pushed the help button and screamed for the nurses to come check on her.

Two nurses rushed into the room to see what she was screaming about.

"She moved! She's moving!" Ms. Moore yelled.

"Calm down, you don't want to startle her. I'll call the doctor immediately," the youngest nurse confirmed.

Moments later the handsome doctor reached the room to ease all the tension.

"Everyone please calm down. Nurse can you bring me a new IV and 300mg of Morphine. Also you contact the detectives and have them contact me."

Precisely he began to check all of her vital signs and wounds by talking to her for certain reactions. Stacy responded to all the commands as her mother observed.

"Is she out of the coma, Doctor?" she asked.

"Yes, it seems she's having a little difficulty breathing on her own and remembering her body functions. I'll run several test on her and over the next few hours, I'll check back in on her," he stated.

"That's good. Oh, thank you God," Ms. Moore said aloud.

"Yes it is. I have to make a few calls so stay by her side," he said.

Ms. Moore was extremely excited and called Kim and Joey's family to tell them the good news. Several hours later Kim and Rondo arrived to bring Ms. Moore lunch and to check on their friend.

Outside in the parking lot the Detectives scanned over the case file and prepared the questions they had to ask Stacy. They had waited a long time to get the information they needed to solve this case. They went inside and the doctor briefed them on Stacy's condition and gave them 10 minutes with her because they didn't want to stress her.

They walked into the room and were greeted by Ms. Moore. "Hello, Detectives."

"We're happy to hear the good news. You do know that one she is fully awake we'll need to ask her a few questions," Freeman stated.

"Is she in any trouble?" Ms. Moore asked concerned.

"No, not at all. We just need to get a little information to close the file," Detective Ross said.

Ms. Moore agreed with a slight nod, then kissed Stacy on the forehead.

Over the next few hours everyone stayed at the hospital. The nurses paid close attention to her vitals and the dosage of medicine that they doctor had recommended be administered.

Ms. Moore was in the waiting room when the nurse came in to tell her that Stacy had finally opened her eyes. Everyone who was there waiting with her rushed into the room to see her finally awake.

Stacy's mind was cloudy as she tried to focus on all the figures in the room. She slowly began to recognize the faces.

"Hey honey bunch," her mom said softly.

"We love you Stacy," Kim whispered.

Stacy looked scared as she wondered how she had survived the incident and how bad was the damage.

"Joey? Joey? Where is Joey?" she asked in a parched voice when she noticed he wasn't in the room.

"Calm down honey," Ms. Moore said rubbing her hair.

"Momma, no! Please tell me he's alive!" she cried.

Nobody wanted to tell her the news but all their faces told her anyway. Every last persons eyes were filled with tears of agony for her.

The doctor asked that everyone leave the room. He explained to Stacy her injuries and that she needed to calm down and get some rest. The nurses would come and change her bandages shortly. He gave her something to help her rest.

All of her visitors sat down in the waiting room playing catch up as she slept. They sat for hours before Kim and Rondo went to the car for a smoke break.

In the parking lot they rolled up a blunt and talked about the recovery of their friend. Kim passed the blunt to Rondo when they noticed a large black SUV pulling out of a parking spot nearby. They both recalled seeing the truck before as they focused on the vehicle. The truck suddenly sped towards them as Rondo reached for his stash to get his gun but it was too late.

A gunman leaned out of the passenger side door with an AK-47 and let off hundreds of rounds into the parked vehicle. The two never had a chance as the truck sped off toward the freeway eluding the police.

The gunshots were loud enough to be heard inside the hospital as hospital security ran out the entrance. Detective Freeman and Ross rushed outside to see Kim and Rondo being placed on rolling beds and hauled off into the emergency room.

Detective Freeman pulled two guards over to him and told them to get to the sixth floor right away and do not let anyone leave or enter the room.

It was chaotic outside the hospital as the police tried to secure the crime scene. While bystanders were gawking at the bloody scene as officers tried to get some order.

Detective Freeman and Ross finally made it back up to Stacy's room where she and her mother were talking.

"Ok you two remain on post until told otherwise," Detective Ross ordered the guards.

"Is everything ok?" Ms. Moore asked.

"Ms. Moore we need to talk to your daughter, asap!" he said frowning.

"What's the problem is everything alright?" she asked standing up.

"No, you daughters two visitors were just gunned down in the parking lot in broad day light at a fucking hospital, for Christ sake!" he shouted.

Stacy looked up and covered her mouth in shock.

"They are being worked on as we speak but we need some answers to avoid any more harm coming to anyone else," Detective Ross said.

"I'm ready," Stacy said quietly.

After 30 minutes of explaining the last few years of her life in detail, everyone was in complete shock. Detail for detail she pointed out to the detectives as her mom couldn't believe her ears. They figured the shooting was retaliation of some sort Terrance's friends. Since they knew who he really was now that Stacy was awake, it would be easier to locate his family and associates.

When she finally finished, the detectives rose up to leave to pursue the information she had given them. Stacy was in tears as she realized that Joey was really gone and now her two friends had been shot.

"All this is happening because of my own bad decision," replayed over and over in her mind. The mental anguish was affecting her physically as she reached on the side of the bed to release some more medicine in her IV.

Her mother and the detectives were standing in the doorway talking when the doctor came in. "I'm glad you all are still here. I have some good news and unfortunately some bad news as well."

"Give us the bad news," Stacy suggested feeling drowsy from the medicine.

"Your friend Kim didn't survive her injuries, Stacy. I'm sorry. However Rondo, was hit several times but he is in stable condition in the ER," the doctor explained.

Ms. Moore and Stacy held hands and cried as he continued, "The good news is that you are two and half months pregnant, with what looks like twins. Congratulations!"

"Pregnant? Oh my God, I'm pregnant?" she tried to yell.

Ms. Moore looked startled and amazed that the babies had survived the trauma of her being shot. Would they be born healthy?

The doctor answered her question before she asked, "Yes, pregnant with twins and we were able to save them without any major complications," he finished.

Stacy laid in the bed with everyone looking at her as she thought to herself, "I'm pregnant, but which one of them is the father?"

DISCUSSION QUESTIONS

1. DO YOU AGREE WITH STACY AND JOEY'S REALTIONSHIP?

2. AT WHAT POINT DID THINGS GO WRONG?

3. DO YOU THINK RONDO SHOULD HAVE CONVINCED JOEY TO LEAVE STACY?

4. DO YOU THINK JOEY SHOULD HAVE TOLD STACY ABOUT THE CRAZY NIGHT WITH KIM?

5. WAS STACY WRONG FOR HER ACTIONS OR JUST CONFUSED?

6. WAS KIM A GOOD FRIEND TO STACY?

7. WHICH MAN TREATED STACY THE BEST AS A COMPANION?

8. IF YOU WERE JOEY, WOULD YOU HAVE FORGIVEN STACY?

9. SHOULD STACY HAVE TOLD JOEY ABOUT TERRANCE STALKING HER?

10. WHO DO YOU BELIEVE IS THE DADDY OF THE TWINS?